WESTERN BRIDES: CARRIE'S TRUST

PIONEER BRIDES OF THE OREGON TRAIL

INDIANA WAKE

FAIR HAVENS BOOKS

INTRODUCTION

This is the second book exploring the brave and amazing journey that was the famous Oregon Trail.

As I promised I will share a little of my research on the trail in each book.

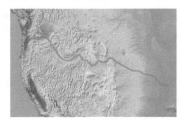

The Oregon Trail is a 2170 mile wagon route that connected the Missouri River to Oregon.

It was laid by fur traders from around 1811 to 1840. Originally only passable on foot or horseback by 1836 a wagon trail had been cleared to Fort Idaho and eventually to Willamette Valley in Oregon.

Annual improvements were made as more and more people took to the trail. It was used by nearly 400,000 settlers, miners, ranchers, farmers and their families.

In this part I will answer a few of your questions.

What did they eat on the Oregon Trail?

This question was asked by the most of my readers. There wasn't much room to carry provision on the wagon, or Prairie Schooner. After all one wagon had to carry everything you needed for the journey and to set up your future.

Staples such as lard, flour, cornmeal, salt and bacon would be carried and they had guns to bring down wild game, venison, buffalo or turkey where ever they fund the time to shoot. Biscuits would be cooked and eaten with meat and gravy as well as any berries and vegetables they could find. If they were lucky they had a cow for milk and a few chickens to lay eggs.

Meat would be charred to preserve it. They would then eat down to the fresh meat and char it the following night to preserve it further.

It was a hard life and one where they had to make the most of what they had but these were ingenious people who knew how to survive.

What would you miss if you had to take such a trip?

This is a standalone book about a group of people who traveled west along the Oregon Trail and the lives they had once they arrived.

The first book was <u>Trinity's Loss</u> and you can read it here <u>http://amzn.to/2xrn4B5</u>

To receive two free Mail Order Bride Romance join Fair Havens Books exclusive newsletter. <u>http://eepurl.com/bHou5D</u>

God bless,

Indiana Wake

CHAPTER 1

"Oh, Joseph, I thought this day would never come," Carrie Easter said, while laughing and crying all at once. She threw her arms around her brother's neck and clung on to him tightly.

"Well, just look at you, all those miles and all that hardship and you're still as pretty as a picture." Joseph tried to sound jovial, although the emotion in his voice was clearly noticeable.

"And this here is Dillon Goodman." Carrie nodded towards the man who stood beside him. "We met at the camp at Independence and he was kind enough to carry my belongings in his wagon and keep me safe throughout the journey." Carrie, feeling emotional herself, blinked rapidly to disperse the build-up of tears. "And Dillon, this is my brother, this is Dr. Joseph Easter." She stood back a little to allow the two men to shake hands vigorously.

"It sure is nice to meet you, Dr. Easter. Your sister here has told me so much about you already." Dillon Goodman smiled amiably. "She really was no trouble at all, in fact, she made the long journey much more enjoyable."

Carrie knew that she would never be able to properly express to him exactly how grateful she was for his kindness throughout so hard a journey.

"And I owe you a debt of gratitude, Mr. Goodman, for taking such good care of my sister. When she wrote me from the camp in Missouri to tell me that you'd offered her assistance over the Oregon Trail, you sure did put my mind at rest."

"It was a pleasure, Doc." Dillon was grinning but backing away slightly and Carrie knew that he was getting ready to take his leave. "And let me tell you, without your sister and the other two ladies who travelled with us, I'd never have got my wagon through the mud and high waters of the last few miles. You have a sister to be proud of there. Sir, she pushed that wagon alongside me and the others, almost up to her knees in mud. She's got a lot of determination."

"She certainly has, Mr. Goodman." Joseph was grinning also, pleased to finally meet the man to whom he did, indeed, owe a debt of gratitude. "Don't you be a stranger now, I've got a very good housekeeper and she cooks real nice. You see you come over for your dinner whenever you can."

"Now, that is an offer that I can't refuse, Sir." Dillon inclined his head with a smile. "Now, I reckon I'm going to let the two of you catch up while I head back down the road a piece and sort my wagon out."

"Thank you, Dillon," Carrie said, her eyes now filling with tears, which she could no longer hold back.

"And thank you, Carrie." Dillon stood for a moment and seemed as if he didn't quite know what to do next.

However, Carrie, unable to stop herself, flung her arms around his neck and hugged him tightly, tears of gratitude rolled down her cheeks and spread out between them, and a multitude of other emotions passed through her.

As Carrie watched him slowly walk away, wiping her tears from his cheeks she knew her tears hid his own. He walked off to his own wagon and the makeshift camp on the edge of town. There he was planning to set up his well-used cotton tent once again, and she could hardly believe that she had made it.

It seemed so long ago that they had set off from Independence, Missouri, and embarked upon the easiest few miles of the Oregon Trail. If she had known then of all that they were to face along the way, Carrie knew that she would not have felt anywhere near as optimistic and excited as she had in those early days. Still, she was there now, finally reunited with the brother she loved. She had missed him terribly for the last year since he had made that wonderful, terrible, arduous journey himself.

* * *

"WELL, you come right on in, Carrie, and see your new home," Joseph said brightly, tactfully not mentioning her tears at all as he shouldered the last of her many and varied belongings into the house.

The house was much bigger than she had been expecting, and it looked wonderfully new, its wood so clean and without a blemish, freshly painted in a spotless, bright white. From the front it certainly looked wide, with many windows and two large doors. As they stood just inside the first door, Carrie's face was wide with amazement.

"The other door is the one to the surgery," Joseph said when he saw her looking at it inquisitively. "As I said in my letters, I separated the surgery from the main part of the house a little, and it even has its own door from the road. But enough of that for now, let's get you inside and get you rested before I give you the big tour." Joseph laughed.

Carrie threw her arms around Joseph and squeezed tightly. She could never have wished for a better brother. At thirty, Joseph was five years older than her. He had always treated her with the greatest admiration, even when they were young and Carrie was just a child. They never bickered like most siblings but rather, they always had so much in common. They enjoyed the same interests and laughed at the same curiosities of life.

When Joseph had first decided to make his move to Oregon, Carrie had wanted to go with him immediately. However, Joseph had insisted that she remain in Missouri, in the house that they had grown up in. The house that their father had left them when he passed away just two years before.

Joseph had wanted to make sure that there really was a chance for a new and exciting life in Oregon before he sent for his sister to join him there.

He had written to her every week, a steady stream of letters. Even though many of them took many weeks to arrive, each one of them, long and full of wonderful descriptions to make the distance between them seem very much shorter than it truly was. When he had written to her that the practice had grown to such an extent that he thought they really could make a good life in Oregon, Carrie knew that the time had come and she could hardly wait to get there.

"Joseph, this is lovely. It's so homely and so comfortable."

Carrie walked through a large sitting room with neat, comfortable couches and all sorts of soft furnishings that she approved of entirely. "It's as homely as the old place, Joseph. I know Daddy would have been real proud to see it."

"I'm glad you like it." Joseph smiled sadly. "And there's a whole lot more to see. And I've given you the biggest bedroom too, I know how you like space."

"Joseph, I really have missed you so much," Carrie said with a great sigh, remembering just how kind and thoughtful her brother really was. "Can I see my room?" She spoke with a little excitement and was pleased to see that Joseph appreciated it.

"Of course, come on." He took her hand and led her through the sitting room and back out into the hallway they had just come through.

As he led her up the wide, wooden staircase, Carrie's head turned this way and that as she tried to take in every detail of her new home. When they reached her bedroom, Carrie could see that it really was large, perhaps even larger than the one she had enjoyed in their old home.

The bed had pretty covers on it. Close by was a wooden dressing table painted white, with a large, oval mirror sitting on top of it. There were chests of drawers and a small table by her bed with a huge vase of fall blooms in it.

"Joseph, everything is so perfect." Carrie turned to hug her brother again. "Everything is so neat and tidy and I'm the one standing out now as tired and dirty." She laughed.

"Don't you worry about that, Dana is already warming water on the stove and getting a bath filled for you. Once you've had something to eat, a bath, and a rest, you'll be as good as new."

They returned downstairs and Carrie sat at a huge wooden kitchen table. Meanwhile, Dana, the housekeeper, set out some bread, butter, and cheese for her, all to be washed down with strong, hot coffee.

Dana was a pleasant young woman of around seventeen or eighteen years of age and she seemed so pleased to meet Carrie finally that Carrie was almost overwhelmed.

When Dana was once again busy with heating water, and ferrying it through to a little room next door set aside for just that purpose, Joseph joined Carrie at the table as she ate.

"You know, now that I'm eating and I'm sitting down and my journey is over, I feel suddenly exhausted." Carrie smiled as she chewed the wonderfully heavy, tasty bread.

"It's quite an ordeal, the Oregon Trail, isn't it?"

"It sure is, Joseph. But I'm so glad to be here, so glad that you finally sent for me."

"Well, business is booming for me. I guess I have more patients than I can cope with already and I needed another doctor to share the load. I knew I couldn't wait another year for the next wagon train to come this way." He laughed.

"But I'm not a real doctor, am I?" She said sadly, the familiar disappointments of life rolling over her.

"You are a real doctor, Carrie. You know as much as I know, and you can do as much as I can do." Joseph, as always, defended her medical prowess.

"You are always so kind, Joseph."

"On this occasion, sister, it isn't kindness, just common sense. I really do need you here."

"You could have hired an assistant."

"I could have, there's plenty of women here in the town who would be able to provide real good, practical nursing care. But I needed another doctor, somebody I can rely on completely. There's only one person I can think of who fits the bill."

"Well, you'd probably better not tell the rest of the town you think of me as a doctor. You don't want to start losing patients now that you have them."

"We'll take it little by little." He smiled. "And just as soon as Boston or Pennsylvania offer up real training for women, I'll be sending you right over there. I'll take on an assistant then, and not before."

Carrie and Joseph's father, Dr. Isaac Easter, had trained them both in medicine from the moment they had each been able to understand. Isaac had never made any distinction between his son and daughter, seeing that they were both equally skilled in the field and equally knowledgeable.

By the time Joseph had been sent to college to complete his medical training, there was not a great deal that he did not know already. He had been helping his father in every practical sense for some years before he had ever sat an exam, as had Carrie. However, Carrie had not enjoyed the same privilege of college and a formal education in medicine.

But her father, a man who never once doubted her talents, had set aside a large portion of their joint inheritance that was to be used solely for her medical training once the world had *finally caught up*, as he put it.

Isaac had been a renowned physician, a man of learning who had always kept up with his training, never assuming that he knew all there was to know. As a result, he had kept an ear to the ground at all times in hopes that attitudes would change and his daughter, who had worked so hard to gain so much knowledge and skill, would one day be recognized.

Shortly before he had died, Isaac Easter had heard rumblings, as he called them, rumors that women might soon be able to take their place in the halls of learning. He was certain that training establishments in either Boston or Pennsylvania would be offering places to women like Carrie before his years were over. But sadly, Isaac had died before ever knowing if those rumblings would come to anything. And there was many a time that Carrie doubted that they ever would.

"Joseph, you sound as sure as Daddy was that I would one day have what you have."

"Because I know that Daddy was right, change is coming, and I keep hearing things from my old friends back East to give me hope for the future. You just hold tight to that, Carrie, because I know that the world *will* catch up, just as Daddy said it would."

"So, have you had anybody stay in your infirmary yet?" Carrie said brightly, her belly full of bread and cheese and a sleepy feeling beginning to wash over her.

"No, not yet. I tried to put it off, waiting for you, really. I don't think I could manage the four beds that I've put in on my own and keep consulting at the same time. I've been lucky that there hasn't been much need for a long-term patient. But I reckon that we could work it between us, what do you think?"

"I think I can't wait to get started, Joseph." Carrie smiled, determined not to let her fears for the future, her own future in medicine, cloud the wonderful day.

"Then I'll show you around everything tomorrow. As I said, there's only four beds, but I've got a lot of new instruments and ideas that I want to show you. It all still needs organizing if we really are going to keep space here for the worst cases, which is where you come in, really."

"Now, you know fine well that you're just as organized as I am, Joseph," Carrie said, laughing despite being grateful for the praise.

"Maybe, but it just wasn't the same without you. We'll work together, two Dr. Easters under one roof."

"If you say so, Joseph." Carrie smiled warmly. "But you really will have to take it slowly. Folk still don't like women doing jobs that they see as too important for them to cope with. And they don't care if the woman has a talent or not, they just can't let themselves believe it."

Carrie's talents had been tested more than once on the Oregon Trail. She had tended to no end of minor injuries and ailments, not to mention some dreadful accidents and much more serious illnesses. And her successes and failures had been met with mixed opinions, as many negative as there were positive. Even people she helped had, on occasion, behaved without a shred of gratitude for either her assistance or her knowledge.

Of course, there were others, people such as Dillon Goodman, who always described her as a doctor whenever he found somebody for her to help on the wagon train. He was one of those rare beings who seemed to take such ideas in his stride, never questioning it or doubting it. Once he had seen for himself how talented she truly was.

And there were others along the way who had been just like him, people who could see beyond everything they had ever been told, every lie and every bigoted judgement, and simply accept her for who she was and what she could do.

Those had been the days which had always fortified her, always given her hope that the future her father had foreseen for her would one day come. Those were the days she knew that she must cling to, for there would, undoubtedly, be negative times to come.

"I promise you, Carrie, we'll just take it day by day. All will be right, just you wait and see." Joseph smiled and turned as Dana came back into the kitchen to announce that the bath was all done, whenever Carrie was ready for it.

For her first day, at least, Carrie would simply relax and enjoy herself, staving off any little fears and worries which would seek to attach themselves to her.

CHAPTER 2

*C*arrie had been surprised by how quickly she had recovered from the trials and tribulations of the Oregon Trail. The whole thing had been such a physical experience that she knew she was stronger and had much more stamina about her than she had ever experienced before.

The stamina and strength that Carrie had gained on that long hard road was welcomed, and she hoped she could hold onto it if at all possible.

The first few days at her new home had been wonderful, and her hopes and spirits has risen with each hour that passed. She had got to grips with the house, which was large and every bit as impressive as it had been when she first saw it. She had already spent a couple of days familiarizing herself with the inner workings of the successful practice that her brother had already built up.

Carrie had, of course, rearranged his filing, which had never been particularly impressive. Joseph hadn't minded a bit, and she couldn't help but think that he had fully expected that she would have some input on that subject the moment she arrived in Oregon.

The little infirmary that Joseph had made out of a large room with four beds, a clean and bright table for minor surgeries, and lots of wonderful new equipment, was probably the thing that Carrie had been most impressed with of all. Since it had yet to be used, it felt like a part of life in Oregon that could belong, a little at least, to Carrie. Joseph told her to set the beds out better if she had a plan that she thought would work more efficiently than his, and she had taken him at his word.

Joseph knew, of course, exactly how his sister operated and dealt with things. He knew that she would enjoy the feeling of coming in at the beginning; and rearranging the infirmary, as yet unused, would be a wonderful way of making it as much hers as it was his.

On that day, as Carrie set about reorganizing the infirmary just how she thought it ought to be, the sun shone brightly through the windows. It was a cool, fall day, but it was just about the brightest she had seen for a while. Something about the way the sunlight poured across the room, bright here, shaded there, made her feel light and optimistic.

She had just begun to change the brand-new white linens on each of the beds, strangely enjoying the somewhat mundane task. Carrie had always liked to work, had always liked to be busy, and making up beds was as good as anything as far as she was concerned. And it was all to a good end, for their little infirmary would soon be up and running.

As she worked away, humming to herself, Carrie could hear some movement and talking in the doctor's consulting rooms adjacent to the infirmary. She recognized her brother's voice, of course, but there was another male voice she had never heard before. At first, she simply assumed that it was a patient and decided to keep out of the way to afford the man some privacy while he consulted his doctor.

However, the voices grew louder and she knew that they were approaching the infirmary itself.

"Ah, here she is." Joseph said, smiling brightly as he looked at her and then back at his companion.

"Yes, here I am, making beds." Carrie smiled at her brother and turned to look at the stranger.

He was a little older than Joseph, at perhaps thirty-two or thirty-three years. The man had dark hair, so dark it was almost black but not quite. And he had a neat, closely trimmed beard to match. Even from a few feet away, Carrie could see that the man's eyes were a wonderful, bright blue. They stood out so well against his dark hair and beard that she thought they were quite striking.

"Carrie, let me introduce you to my dear friend, Mr. Daniel Macey." Joseph looked so pleased to be able to introduce them.

"Of course, Mr. Macey, how lovely to meet you. I have heard of you already in my brother's many letters." Carrie put down the sheet she was unfolding and hastened across the room.

She held her hand out tentatively to Daniel Macey, and he took it in his own, shaking it quite vigorously.

"Your brother talks of you all the time, Miss Easter, so I must admit that I feel as if I know you already. And it sure is good to finally meet you after all this time." He smiled and Carrie thought it made him very handsome. It was a bright smile, wide and warm.

"And it's good to finally meet you, Mr. Macey. From what I hear, you have been a very good friend to my brother."

"I guess we kind of propped each other up a little bit over this last year. We met early on, in the first few miles of the trail. Having said that, there were only a few of us and by the end of it, I reckon we all knew each other like family."

"Yes, my brother tells me that there were barely one hundred of you."

"Whereas there were a thousand of you." Daniel Macey looked impressed. "Even now, I can hardly imagine what that looked like. It must sure have been a sight to see so many wagons travelling together."

"I must admit it was. Especially in the beginning when everything was still exciting and nothing bad had happened. Back then, *everything* was so impressive. Especially at night, when the wagons were circled. You can imagine what so many wagons in circles looked like, Mr. Macey."

"I think that was the part of it all that I liked best. You know, with a long day's walking and riding behind you, and an evening of rest and music and a good meal. It makes for good friendships, something like that." He nodded thoughtfully. "But I guess, being fewer of us, we didn't see as many of the tragedies that you will have seen."

"There certainly were tragedies enough, Mr. Macey. I had never even contemplated how many people who started off on that journey with us wouldn't make it to Oregon." She spoke sadly.

Carrie was instantly transported back several months to the

beginning of their journey. When she had first befriended Dillon Goodman at the camp at Independence, Missouri, she had thought it would all be so much simpler from there.

Dillon had been a nice man, young, and so full of enthusiasm. And he had been a popular fellow, with so many people taking to him with ease. And the more she talked to him of her old life, of how much her father had taught her, the more he found stray folk along the way who needed her help.

At first, there had been so many minor ailments and injuries that Carrie had been happily diverted, pleased to be able to help, and pleased to have something a little different to do which would clearly mark one day from another as they continued on, ever forward.

Then had come that awful night when she had heard a woman screaming and moaning. It was the unmistakable sounds of labor, and she knew that somewhere in the tents inside the circled wagons, was a woman in need of assistance.

John and Leonora Shepherd were a kindly couple, young and full of hope for the future. They were five or six years younger than Carrie, probably not yet twenty, and they had decided upon a life of farming in Oregon.

Leonora had been pregnant before the start of the journey, but the exuberance of youth had not stopped them from setting off. They had even thought that they might make it all the way to Oregon before she finally gave birth, and yet it was not to be. Leonora had gone into labor early and had struggled terribly. By the time Carrie had reached her, the baby was already out and she did what she could to clean them both up and make sure that the baby was healthy and comfortable.

But the labor had taken its toll on Leonora. She had lost a lot of blood. Within an hour of her baby taking that first breath, Leonora Shepherd's heart had given out, and she had passed away before they had even made it as far as Independence Rock.

"Carrie?" Joseph said when she had been silent for some moments.

"Forgive me, I'm afraid I was back on the Oregon Trail for a while there."

"It takes a good piece of time to get it out of your system, Miss Easter, so don't you worry about it. Even now, some of the days and some of the nights come back to me with full force. To be honest, it's almost every night I close my eyes." Daniel smiled at her and she thought he instantly understood that time of sadness.

"It's a shame to say, that there was so much excitement and hope, and even fun and laughter, and yet it is the saddest things that come back to you," Carrie said with a shrug. "I was thinking of a man who lost his wife in childbirth. They were both so young."

"Isn't that the man who is setting up a farm on the land he claimed? I know there is a man on his own with a small baby, because he came into have me take a look at her," Joseph said gently.

"Yes, yes," Carrie said and nodded. "His name is John Shepherd and he has a baby daughter."

"That's real tough," Daniel said, re-joining the conversation. "Can't be easy for a man to try to get a farm up and running when he's got a baby under his arm."

"No, it can't." Carrie was pleased to be talking to somebody who seemed to care. But, of course, any man who had managed to befriend her brother so completely could surely only be a good man. "But I have already been speaking to Trinity, the young woman I travelled along with. Between us, we're hoping to be able to entreat a small team of Townswomen to help him with the baby until he gets on his feet."

"Well, that sure is nice of you." Daniel Macey smiled at her and nodded. "And I reckon the poor man will be real appreciative."

"And it's a good place," Joseph said hopefully. "There's not many here who don't have a good idea of how hard it was to get here. To many, helping others has become second nature. I guess it had to be on that journey, didn't it?"

"It sure did. I have no doubt that we'll all look back in years to come and recognize how the Oregon Trail changed us." Daniel looked at her intently and Carrie couldn't help but think that his words already meant so much. He was absolutely right, of course, that nobody could fail to be changed by travelling overland on the Oregon Trail. Changed for the good, predominantly, she was sure, but changed nonetheless. And of course, there were people whose lives had changed beyond repair, people like Trinity, and her mother, who had lost a father and husband in one dreadful moment. "But I guess some of the changes were lessons, things which have taught us all how to give an eye to the lives of others." Daniel finished and then looked around the infirmary. "Looks like you're doing a real good job here, Miss Easter."

In truth, Carrie was glad for his sudden change of direction. She felt that all three of them had been transported just a little and that the conversation was having a deep effect on them all. It seemed to Carrie that the conversation had become too deep too quickly, although she thought it curious that she had not been made uncomfortable by it.

"Well, my brother has allowed me to change things around a little, instill a little order here and there." Carrie smiled shyly.

"Allowed her? I wouldn't dare stop her." Joseph laughed.

"No, from everything your brother has told me, I'm sure you'll be making a real big difference to his life here, at home and work."

"That's real nice of you to say so, Mr. Macey."

"Why don't you just go on ahead and call me Daniel? After all, if you're anything like your brother, I'm sure that we'll be real good friends in no time."

"I'm sure of it too. And you must call me Carrie." For reasons she could not explain, Carrie could feel her cheeks flush a little.

She suddenly felt curiously tongue-tied and hoped that her brother would soon put an end to the little meeting and let her get on with her work. Not that she wouldn't have happily spent a little more time with Daniel Macey, but she just wanted a bit of time and space to gather herself and examine her thoughts a little. She wanted to know why it was that she had reacted so to his friendliness. After all, it wasn't like she hadn't seen a handsome man before, and yet none of them had ever rendered her just this side of speechlessness.

"Well, Carrie, I guess I'd better let you get on with it," Daniel smiled, seeming not to notice her sudden shyness. "And again, it was real nice to meet you."

"You too, Daniel."

"And you'll come for dinner this week, Daniel? Dana has promised to cook us up something special and you know what a good cook she is." Joseph, seemingly unaware of his sister's slight disquiet, carried on regardless. "Wednesday, what do you say?"

"Sounds perfect, Joe." Daniel nodded and reached out to shake Joseph by the hand. "I'll sure look forward to another one of Dana's wonderful meals. And I'll look forward to seeing you again too, Carrie." He turned to give her one final, devastatingly handsome smile, before bidding them both good day and making his way out of the infirmary.

"What a nice man," Carrie said, feeling she ought to at least say something.

"He's one of the best, Carrie. I sure am glad to finally have the two of you meet." Joseph gave her a conspiratorial grin, and she realized that, despite the fact that he had ignored it, her brother had recognized the little bit of attraction that she had felt for his friend.

CHAPTER 3

"*I* don't know how to thank you ladies enough for everything you're doing." John Shepherd said, his young face aged with grief.

"Well, Suki sure does make it easy, John. She is just the most *adorable* little baby." Trinity cooed over baby Suki. Carrie watched the care that Trinity took over the handling of the baby, and was impressed for a woman so young and without a child of her own.

The both of them barely twenty-years-old, they had each suffered the most appalling losses in their young lives, and in most traumatic ways. And yet they were both bright and determined to make the very best of life, to keep going.

John Shepherd really was a lesson in keeping going. Carrie would never forget his heart-breaking cries on the night his daughter had been born and his beloved wife had died. Now here he was, just months later, continuing with the plan that he and Leonora had made not a year before. He was intent on building up the flourishing farm that he and his childhood sweetheart had been so sure would be theirs.

Quite how he could keep going when his partner in all of it was no longer there, Carrie could not imagine.

"She really is a lovely baby, John. And we've managed to get quite a queue of Townswomen all keen to help out, so you need not worry about that anymore. You'll have the time now to get out there and get your farm up and running and, once you start turning a profit, I'm sure you will be able to get somebody in on a permanent basis." Carrie concentrated on the practicalities for fear that she would, otherwise, dissolve into tears of emotion.

"I couldn't do it without this help," John said simply, and Carrie blinked hard. "I would never manage it, but I promise you, I won't be relying on people's kindness forever. As you say, Doc, as soon as I have his place up and running, I'll get someone in. I won't dawdle, I'll get on with it."

"We know that, honey," Trinity said kindly. "And today is the first day of it all. You can get out there and start organizing things and do whatever you need to do because Mrs. Jeannie Stanton will be here with Suki."

"Yes, I met her already and she's real nice," John said with an enthusiastic smile.

"And she sure does love babies," Trinity said and Carrie thought the woman sounded perfect.

Carrie had not yet met Jeannie Stanton, but Trinity had made a great friend of her already, as she had done of many of the local women. Trinity had a bright and attractive personality and a very open nature which drew people in almost immediately. In truth, Carrie wished she had a little of Trinity's magic about her.

"That's real nice." John said quietly. "I just hope that Suki wakes up in time to greet Mrs. Stanton when she arrives." He looked down doubtfully at the sleeping baby.

She was in a tiny crib in the one room that John planned to rent until he had his land in order and his little house built. He was sticking to the plan that he and Leonora had made, sticking to it rigidly, despite the fact that she was no longer there.

"Well, she should be along in about an hour, John," Trinity said. "And then you can get out there and start building a wonderful life for you and little Suki."

When they left the small, cramped little room and headed out into the pale, late fall sunshine, Carrie felt relieved that she had not cried in John's presence. She had never quite recovered herself from the fact that so young a woman had died and that there had been nothing she could do about it. Yet, John had never once blamed her for it, always referring to her as *Doc*. She had no doubt that other men, had their wives died in her presence, would have taken the easy path to anger and blamed it all on her.

In a nutshell, Carrie supposed that *that* was what frightened her most about openly treating people, openly working as a doctor. Even if things did change and she finally ended up at Boston or Pennsylvania, returning home with her medical credentials in her hand, people would still view her with that curious suspicion, the idea that she could not possibly be as effective as a man.

"He just gets on with it, doesn't he?" Trinity broke the dreary gloom that had descended about Carrie's shoulders.

"Yes, he is quite remarkable. He's so young, and he's already lost so much." Carrie shook her head from side to side.

"But he's not alone. We've got plenty of women keen to help him out and help him find his way. He sure is determined."

"Yes, he is. I guess there is a lesson to be learned there." Carrie spoke gently.

"You mean for yourself?" Trinity gently prodded.

"I suppose so. I must admit, on the way here, to *be* here was all that I wanted. To be with my brother and to start practicing medicine properly again. But I have these doubts, these little fears that won't leave me alone. And as small as they are, they keep at me, almost leaving me with the idea that I shouldn't even attempt it. That I should be content to keep my brother's files and make the beds, and stay far away from the job I love."

"And then you see John and you remember that you *have* to try it, no matter what." Trinity sounded quite vehement.

"Yes, I see my own little concerns and then I look at John and I feel ashamed."

"You have nothing to feel ashamed for, Carrie. And your concerns aren't little, they're big. The fight that you have on your hands is a very different one from John's, but it's a fight nonetheless. It's one that I know you can win. Anyone who makes it across the Oregon Trail, as far as I'm concerned, can do anything they put their mind to. Let's not forget, your mind is already full of everything you know, so you have a head start."

"Thank you." Carrie said, feeling fortified by the young woman's words.

"And I think I actually have a patient for you, I meant to tell you before," Trinity said and slowed her pace for a moment.

"You do?" Carrie was intrigued. "I mean, so far I've only hung about the surgery and seen people coming in and out. They all know me as the doctor's sister and that is it."

"Yes, but Jeannie Stanton seemed very interested when I told her a little about you. When I told her that you had all the knowledge of a doctor, she asked me if I thought that you would see her. She says she wants to talk to somebody about some kind of changes she's going through, and she thinks she would really prefer to speak to a woman about it all than a man."

"That's quite understandable, really. Nobody ever considers that side of things when they confidently assert that the only people suitable for medical practice are men." Carrie tried to keep the little snap of bitterness out of her voice. "But you think she really would want to come and see me?"

"Well, that's what she asked me to ask you. Shall I bring her to you, maybe tomorrow?"

"Yes, any time tomorrow." Carrie said and felt suddenly excited. "I'll make sure I'm in the surgery all day, you just come along any time you like."

"Well, that's just great, thank you, Carrie."

"No, thank you, Trinity." Carrie reached for Trinity's hand and squeezed it. "I can't tell you what it means to me."

"Maybe all it takes is just one patient." Trinity grinned. "And for that patient to talk about you and then you get another patient, and another, and another."

"So, what does the rest of your day hold?"

"I'm going to go look for Dillon, just to see what he's up to." Trinity smiled as she always did when she talked of Dillon.

Carrie had seen the attraction between the two of them within days of embarking on the Oregon Trail. They both had such sunny outlooks that it seemed inevitable that they would be drawn towards one another. It saddened Carrie to see how their love had been put to one side after the dreadful tragedy which had taken Trinity's father from her on the Rocky Mountain pass.

"He's always so busy." Carrie said with a broad smile. "He's a real worker, isn't he?"

"He sure is." Trinity's cheeks turned little pink as she talked of him. "But what about the rest of your day? Are you going back to the surgery?"

"Actually, I'm heading home to start with. My brother's friend is coming over to see him for a while and Dana has baked an apricot pie. We're going to have pie and coffee, the three of us."

"I take it that friend is Daniel Macey." Trinity said, her cheeks returned to their normal color and her smile suddenly became mischievous.

"Yes, he and my brother seem to be very great friends."

"Although, I think there might be an extra attraction now for Mr. Macey." Trinity grinned.

"Trinity!" Carrie said, but could feel her own cheeks now begin to flush. "He's just my brother's friend. They're just like us, they came across the Oregon Trail together and it's made them very close."

"I'm sure it has, but that doesn't mean that Daniel Macey hasn't got an eye for a pretty lady, does it?"

"Trinity, you're impossible." Carrie was trying to fend her off but, at the same time, found herself enjoying the conversation.

She was entertaining the idea of spending more time with Daniel Macey, and she rather liked it. Of course, she had no idea what *he* thought about the whole thing and they had only met on a few occasions. They had only ever crossed paths as a consequence of Daniel and Joseph being in company. Daniel had never made a visit to see her specifically.

"Well, you do make a nice-looking pair. He's so dark and you're so fair. You look really good together."

"You've never seen us together," Carrie said and laughed loudly.

"No, but I've seen you both individually and I can imagine what you would look like side-by-side." Trinity was not ready to give up and Carrie thought her reasoning most amusing.

"I can't argue with you anymore," Carrie said, shaking her head from side to side. "You're too determined."

"I just think he's a good catch." Trinity said, obviously now deciding to take the sensible route. "An attorney with a little office of his own. And given that he's only been here a year longer than us, he certainly has built a thriving little business, hasn't he?"

"Yes, he sure has. He strikes me as a very clever man."

"So, he's clever, he's handsome, and he has money enough to look after you. Like I said, He's a real good catch." Trinity grinned again.

"I've only known him a couple of weeks, which is hardly long enough to know if we're suited."

"But he came to dinner last week, and now he's coming for pie. Don't be surprised to find out you're as big a draw on his attention as your brother is."

"Well, we shall see. I just don't want to get my hopes up in case I discover that he really is too good to be true," Carrie said sensibly.

"Alright, I'll keep quiet about it for now. For a little while, at least." Trinity smiled brightly. "Well, I'll see you later, I'm heading off down here in search of Dillon."

"You take care now," Carrie said and patted her arm. "And I'll see you tomorrow some time with Mrs. Stanton."

As Carrie began to make her way home, she felt her spirits were lifted greatly. Trinity always had that effect on her, it was true. But also, the idea that she might have her first patient gave her a burgeoning sense of excitement.

Of course, knowing that she would spend another hour or two in the company of Daniel Macey was another cause for excitement, albeit a cautious kind of excitement.

Carrie had enjoyed his company at dinner the week before. He had entered their home brightly and carrying a small bunch of late fall blooms in his arm for the *mistress of the house*, as he'd called her light-heartedly.

Carrie had been worried that she would feel as tongue-tied as she had towards the end of their first meeting, but nothing could have been further from the truth. Daniel was an interesting conversationalist, as was her brother, and the three of them had spent a lively evening.

"And so, you have managed to make quite a legal practice for yourself, Daniel?" Carrie had asked, keen to find out as much about him as possible and thinking that his work was a good place to start.

"I really have, although I was worried at first that moving here, letting go of all the clients I had back in Missouri, might be a mistake. But of course, a brand-new place is full of all sorts of legal wranglings. I'm dealing mostly with land rights at the moment, and with more people coming over the Oregon Trail every year, I reckon there'll be enough of *that* to last the rest of my life if that's what I've a mind to do."

"And yet I'm sensing that you might not be entirely happy with wranglings over land, Daniel." She raised her eyebrows, she had picked up on his tone.

"You're absolutely right, Carrie," he said.

Carrie enjoyed listening to his wonderfully deep voice. And despite its depth, there was something gentle in it, something soothing.

"I must admit Carrie, that I have a great interest in the formation of the burgeoning provisional government here in Oregon. I think it's quite something to see, the beginnings of a place, you know?"

"Yes, despite the fact that I suppose we all come from the same place essentially, the rules might change a little here and there with the development of a whole new society."

"That is exactly it," Daniel said, brightening even more and holding her gaze. "I think it is just interesting to watch as it all unfolds, how people adapt to life here in Oregon and how the rules are all set."

"As hard as it has been to get here, I think that you're right, I think that there are exciting times ahead." Carrie agreed.

"I like the idea of a whole new society." Joseph joined in. "I think it's the perfect opportunity to sweep out old ideas and let the new ones come in." He looked at his sister significantly.

"Perhaps," She said a little shyly.

"There's no perhaps about it, Carrie. Things will change, you just wait and see."

"Maybe they have a little already." She said, suddenly remembering Mrs. Stanton. "I have a lady coming to see me tomorrow for some advice."

"Really? That's wonderful," Joseph said and smiled broadly, raising his coffee cup in toast. "To my sister, the doctor."

"Joseph!" Carrie said, feeling a little embarrassed.

"No, your brother is quite right," Daniel also held his coffee cup aloft. "To Dr. Carrie Easter."

"Well, maybe one day." She smiled and shrugged.

"I'm telling you, Carrie, one day not far from now you'll be packing your bags again and making your way over to Pennsylvania or Boston, I just know it."

"Perhaps." She said and shook her head. "Daniel, you must forgive my brother his enthusiasm. He is absolutely convinced, as my father was, that women would soon be studying medicine in one of those two places."

"Then I'm sure you will," Daniel said and smiled at her, his blue eyes bright against his dark hair. "And I'd be real happy for you. Although I think I would be sorry to see you leave." He smiled at her and she felt her cheeks flush a little.

When she turned to look at her brother, she could see a knowing smile on his face.

CHAPTER 4

*A*s the weeks passed, Carrie developed quite a following of women of a certain age. Trinity had been right; Jeannie Stanton was just the start of things. When Trinity had brought her into the surgery to see her, Carrie could never have imagined her simple care and understanding would have opened the gates for so many more to come her way.

"It's the heat which gets me more than anything, Miss Easter." Jeannie Stanton had told her quietly as the two of them sat in her brother's consulting room. "And I don't mean the heat of the day, I mean the heat inside me. Just out of the blue I suddenly feel as if I've burst into flames, just like that. And I feel like I can't escape from it, I can't cool down, and it makes me feel angry sometimes. Poor old George doesn't know what to do, I think he's just confused by it. And I'm real confused by it too at times, although I do know it's because of my age. I remember my mama going through it all."

"Yes, it's something that comes to us all in the end. Well, most of us at any rate," Carrie said with a smile. "But there's certainly some things that we can try. In fact, I have some herbs that I can give you straight away and you can take some with you and see how you manage."

"Herbs?"

"Yes, there's still room for herbs and what have you, even these days when we have so many new medicines to try. But I always like to go with what works the best, and I also think that most medicines being investigated and invented by men, some of the problems that we ladies suffer from go ignored for much of the time."

"That's why we need more lady docs, just like you." Jeannie Stanton said, and her eyes seem to fill up with tears.

Carrie realized in that moment, that to be listened to and understood was as much a part of a good treatment as anything. She had no doubt that Jeannie had already tried to explain her symptoms to a male doctor or two and had found herself given such simple and pointless advice as using a fan or wearing a thinner dress.

"Well, maybe one day, huh?" Carrie smiled at her encouragingly. "And in the meantime, I'm going to give you some black cohosh. There are other things we can try if this doesn't work, but I think this is the best starting point. I have spoken to many ladies in the past who had some wonderful results with this. It works very well in calming down the heat." Carrie rose to her feet and made her way across the room to search through the many bottles and containers on the shelves.

She found the black cohosh, largely unused, and began to portion some of it out into a small glass jar for Mrs. Stanton to take with her.

The black cohosh had, in the end, worked very well for Mrs. Stanton, not to mention a number of other women who had slowly but surely been making their way to the door of Dr. Joseph Easter's medical practice and shyly asking for the lady doc.

Joseph had been over the moon, pleased that his sister was being accepted by the women of the town, at least. And not just the women, for one of them had brought her husband with her for moral support and, while there, he had sought some advice from her for a few little ailments of his own.

It was on Mrs. Stanton's third visit that Carrie first became aware of a little unrest over the idea of her giving advice that a doctor might. Mrs. Stanton had come for another prescription of black cohosh, claiming it to be a miracle, and just as they were finishing up, Daniel Macey walked in from the road.

Carrie was just walking Mrs. Stanton to the door, the consultation complete, when Jeannie turned to her with a look of concern on her face.

"You're doing real well here, Doc, but you've ruffled a few feathers." Jeannie had taken to calling her *Doc*, as had many of the other ladies of the town.

"Goodness." Carrie said a little surprised. "Have I really?"

"It's nothing you've done, I guess it's just the changes you've been able to make for us women folk. There's always men who don't like that kind of thing, and it seems as if Bart Thornhill is one of them."

"Bart Thornhill? The wealthy landowner?" Carrie felt suddenly a little dismayed.

"He owns just about everything, not just land. That man

wants his finger in all the pies, and he's real ruthless, so just you mind you watch your back."

"But why would he have any objection? I can't think that I've seen his wife here, have I?"

"No, no, he's a widower. His wife is long gone, and knowing what he's like, I should think she's glad of it." Mrs. Stanton spoke so vehemently that Carrie began to feel truly worried.

"So, why are his feathers so ruffled?"

"I don't know exactly, I guess he just sticks his beak into everything and he's gotten wind of how folks are coming here, and how the ladies are starting to talk of you as a doctor. He is just one of them sort of men who doesn't like that sort of thing."

"Perhaps he is just voicing his opinion." Carrie said hopefully. "And I must say, either here or in Missouri, it's probably not something I haven't already heard."

"I reckon it's a bit more than that, Doc. Muriel Havers told me that she'd heard the old weasel saying he would find a way to put a stop to it. She didn't say any more than that, but that was enough for me." Jeannie Stanton stood with one hand on her hip, her freshly replenished jar of black cohosh in the other hand, and she looked suddenly like a force to be reckoned with. "I wouldn't put anything past that man." She said and nodded significantly.

"Well, thank you for letting me know, Mrs. Stanton. I don't know what I can do about it, but it's always a good thing to know what you're up against, so I appreciate you telling it to me."

"I wasn't so sure, Doc. Really, I didn't want to upset you with it all."

"No, not at all."

"Then I'll see you in a week or two." Mrs. Stanton smiled broadly before turning to take her leave. As she made her way towards the door, Daniel Macey opened it for her. "Thank you kindly, Mr. Macey." She smiled at him in that way that old ladies did to young, handsome men.

"Well," Carrie said and shrugged. "I guess I've made an enemy already." She felt very much more down than she appeared, but she did not want Daniel to have any idea how much the news had affected her.

"That man is trying to involve himself in all sorts of business, just as Mrs. Stanton says. But don't worry about him unduly just yet, Carrie, because he has his work cut out for him with the amount of interference he is running all over town." Daniel laughed and it was clear that he was attempting to cheer her up. "Listen, if you're free for a while, maybe you'd join me down at Mrs. Taplow's diner. She's got a blackberry pie today and it's almost as good as one of Dana's." He grinned.

"Yes, I would like that very much. And I'm very hungry," She said thoughtfully, thinking that it had, indeed, been some time since breakfast.

They walked down towards the diner side-by-side, chattering amiably. However, Carrie could not keep her mind off the idea that Bart Thornhill, probably one of the most powerful and influential men in the town, had taken against her.

They made their way inside the diner and Daniel quickly pulled out a chair for her to sit on.

"It looks kind of busy in here today," Daniel began. "I sure do hope that Mrs. Taplow has got a little of that blackberry pie left." He smiled at her but could clearly sense her distraction. "You're really worried, aren't you?"

"I'm worried because it's everything that I feared, Daniel. More, actually." She looked up in time to see Mrs. Taplow herself hurrying over towards them with a big smile on her face.

"Coffee?" Mrs. Taplow asked, looking at them both, a small pencil in her hand poised over a tiny notebook.

"Yes, please, Mrs. Taplow," Daniel said brightly. "And two pieces of your blackberry pie if there's any left."

"It's the last of it, but it's yours, dear," she said with a broad smile before bustling away again.

"Well, that's one piece of good news at least," Daniel said and grinned.

"Hopefully, it's an omen." Carrie shook her head and laughed.

"I don't think you should worry just yet that Bart Thornhill is going to make too much of a special case out of you. He really is making his opinions known on everything in town and I think I know why."

"Why? He's already wealthy and he has the businesses he wants, why does he need to make everybody else's business his own?"

"Because I think he's trying to worm his way into the provisional government. His wealth certainly helps, that's for sure, but making himself look like some kind of town leader, a man whose opinion counts in all sorts of ways, is another way of getting his foot in the door. That's what men like him do, Carrie. They shout a little bit louder than the others, and slowly but surely, they manipulate other people's opinions to look very much like their own."

"And people's opinions, in terms of women as doctors, are not going to be too difficult to manipulate, are they? As far as I'm concerned, the man's work is almost done for him, isn't it?"

"Maybe it is, but look what you've achieved so far. Look how many opinions you've changed already. Joseph told me just how many ladies come knocking on the surgery door these days, and just how many more of them are starting to bring their husbands along. Nobody who has come to see you has anything but praise for you, and that's the truth."

"And I suppose that's the very thing that has alerted Bart Thornhill to my presence. Maybe he will see this one as an easy fight to win and will push all the harder, knowing that if he can get me to stop treating people, the town will look on him as a man who achieves things. Just the right sort of man for a provisional government, perhaps."

"I daresay that's his thinking, Carrie, but I think it's a good thing that you already have such a good idea of his motives. Knowledge is power, right?" He smiled at her and looked straight into her eyes.

Carrie knew that he was trying to encourage her, and allay her fears all at once, and she couldn't have been more grateful. Even though it wasn't working for the moment. At least he believed in her, and that went a very long way to firming up her resolve to keep going.

They both remained silent for a moment, seemingly unable to look away from each other. His eyes really were quite something and she knew that her cheeks were beginning to flush. In the end, she had to break their gaze, knowing that her embarrassment was clear. She laughed a little as she looked down at the pretty little white tablecloth.

"What's so funny?" he asked in that low, deep voice of his.

"Black cohosh," she said without explanation. She thought that she might well, in that moment, benefit from that fine herb if it could at least take some of the high color out of her cheeks.

"Black cohosh?" Daniel, wrinkled his face in confusion. "What?"

"Really, Daniel, it doesn't matter. It's just something that I prescribe to somebody and I think it works very well on blushing cheeks."

"I see," he said and gave her a long, slow smile. "But I think I like to see your cheeks blushing."

"You do?" she said, her breath became shorter and just a little faster.

"I guess it's just the reaction I've been hoping for, if I'm honest."

In the moment that Carrie could not think of a single thing to say, Mrs. Taplow came bustling back with a small tray containing their coffee and pie. Never had a woman had such perfect timing, as far as Carrie was concerned.

As Mrs. Taplow set their things down on the table and engaged them in light conversation, Carrie felt she had been given a little reprieve. And the moment Mrs. Taplow disappeared, Carrie picked up her fork and set about the blackberry pie, still searching for a diversion.

"You're right, Daniel, this pie is wonderful," she said and

smiled at him, pleased to note that her cheeks had returned to their normal temperature.

"See, I told you." He lifted his coffee cup. "And everything will be alright, Carrie, you just see if isn't. Don't you go spending day and night worrying about Bart Thornhill, you just worry about your patients. And in the meantime, I'll keep my eyes and ears open."

"Thank you, Daniel," she said gently, and felt the warmth of his protection settle down about her.

CHAPTER 5

"I hope Dillon's alright," Carrie said with some concern.

"He's just fine, honey. If he hadn't got on that bronco's back, he wouldn't have pulled every muscle in his body. I'm so pleased it was over so fast," Trinity said, and Carrie could still sense the annoyance.

"I know, I know. It's madness really, but look how much further forward it has brought you both. You can really get on with your life now that you have the money." Carrie smiled.

"I know I should forgive him. And I am so grateful that we now have enough money to realize Dillon's dreams and build the merchant's store and our own home." Trinity closed her eyes and shook her head. "I just can't stop remembering how I felt when I saw Thunder set off with him on his back, that point of no return."

"I reckon as life goes on, as things just get better and better, you'll find some way to forgive him." Carrie chuckled.

"Maybe the minute you move out of that tent and into your lovely new home."

Carrie had enjoyed Dillon and Trinity's wedding celebrations more than anything she had enjoyed in a long time. There had been an air of excitement about it all, and most of the town had turned up to see the two of them; after all, there had been so much talk about the new man who had broken the bucking bronco at last.

"In the meantime, he's still got a muscle or two that gives him an ache. No doubt Joseph is hearing all about it as we speak." Trinity laughed.

Trinity had called into the house when her new husband had gone to consult his doctor. Not only was Carrie pleased that it was nothing serious, but she was pleased to see her dear friend for an impromptu cup of coffee and some chatter.

Suddenly, there came a great commotion and much shouting as the door to the main part of the house flew open and Dillon raced in, his face grey with shock.

"Dillon, what is it?" Trinity said, already on her feet and panicked.

"Come quickly, Carrie, its Joseph." Dillon gasped, breathing so hard it was almost as if he had run for a mile to get there.

Without hesitation, Carrie rose from her seat in the kitchen and ran through the house, out onto the road and in through the surgery door. Dillon was hot on her heels as she raced into the consulting room to see her brother lying lifeless on the floor.

His lips were already turning blue and his body entirely motionless. She dropped to her knees at his side and put her cheek against his mouth, horrified to confirm that he was not breathing.

"He just dropped, not a word, not a pain or anything. He just fell to the floor, Carrie, and I didn't know what to do." Dillon said, panic rising in his voice.

Carrie tried to remain calm as she pushed her fingers into his neck in search of a pulse. When she could find none, she knew what had happened. Joseph had suffered a cardiac arrest, likely brought on by an arrhythmia. It was the same way that their father had died more than two years ago, but neither one of them had ever suspected that Joseph would suffer the same fate, only so much younger.

Carrie immediately began to pound on her brother's chest, in the hope of restarting his heart. She placed two hands in the very center of his chest and began to push them rhythmically, placing much of her weight behind her attempt.

"Come on, Joseph, don't leave me. Don't you dare leave me," she said with tears streaming down her face as she spoke through ragged breaths.

When she leaned forward to place her mouth over his, desperate to breathe some air into his lungs, she felt she could hardly breathe herself. The panic and the exertion had exhausted her already, not one minute into her treatment of him.

Finally managing to get a breath into his body, she leaned back on her haunches and watched as his chest descended again as the air came out. She leaned forward and gave another breath, watching out of the corner of her eye as his chest inflated and then, once again, flattened.

She returned to pumping on his chest, hoping against all hope that she could force his heart to return to its ordinary rhythm. But in her heart, she knew the chances of it were extremely slim. Although being told what to do, she had never yet seen anybody revived with such methods.

And, of course, it was something that she had never had to do before, not to anybody. To find herself in the position of trying such a thing first on one of her own family was the most unbearable feeling on earth. Unbearable, and helpless.

Sweat ran down her back, feeling cold and hot all at the same time, as she continued to fight to save her brother's life. All she could think of was how he was just thirty, a man who had yet to marry, had yet to find the love of his life with which to produce the fine children she had always felt sure she would be an aunt to.

Surely, this couldn't be? Surely, this couldn't happen?

"Joseph, come on," she said, and could hear how raw her voice sounded.

She continued to pound on his chest, pausing only to breathe air into his lungs. Dillon had dropped down by her side, helplessly supporting her with nothing more than his presence, having nothing else to offer.

Carrie was aware of Trinity standing in the room, saying nothing but breathing so hard that she could hear it perfectly, almost feel it as if it were her own breath.

Though she was becoming more and more exhausted, Carrie simply could not give up. She knew, deep in her heart, that her brother was already gone. He had already drifted away from her, taking his place in heaven and very likely looking on with sadness at her desperate attempt.

The very idea of it almost ripped her own heart out of her chest, the idea that she would never again talk with her beloved brother. As she continued to pound, as her breath continued to scream in and out of her own body, she tried to think of their final words together.

They had taken breakfast, as they always did, and Joseph had seemed in perfect health. There had been no fatigue, nothing to indicate the devastating arrhythmia that was to come along and devastate them.

"I think Daniel is right, Carrie. Don't let Bart Thornhill upset you too much just yet. After all, a man as ambitious and as interfering as he is might well have bitten off more than he can chew by involving himself in so much that isn't his business in this town. Don't be downhearted yet, just see how things unfold."

"I suppose you're right, Joseph." She had smiled at him, although she was unconvinced.

"You don't seem so sure." Joseph had smiled at her in such a caring way.

"I'm sorry, I'd like to be more optimistic, but put yourself in my shoes. I can't help but think that he already has a leg up on this, you know how people feel about this sort of thing. You know how people feel about women doing jobs that they think belong only to men. Maybe I'm his easiest target out of all of them."

"Well, I don't know. It's not just you he's gunning for, him and that dreadful son of his are already, I have no doubt, hatching some scheme or other to take the wind out of Dillon Goodman's sails, especially after he married Trinity. They're just that sort of family, the sort that won't let things go, the sort that bear grudges."

"And there you are telling me *not* to worry," she said with a broad grin. "This is a very confused message, Joseph."

"I know, I'm afraid I'm not very good at this sort of thing. But what I do know, what I know for certain, is that you are just about the finest doctor I have ever had the good fortune to work with. There's a really good reason why Daddy was so proud of you, why he set aside so much money to have you sent to college the minute the world *catches up*, remember?"

"If I have nothing else in this world, Joseph, I will always have in my heart the faith that you and Daddy had in me. The faith that you still have. I already have so much more than most, so please forgive me when I allow myself to descend into a little doubt. In the end, I do know that I can do it. But I only know that because you and Daddy always supported me so, and I'll always be grateful for that."

"Well, you just keep that in mind." Joseph had risen to his feet, still chewing on the bread-and-butter he was taking for breakfast. "But in the meantime, I've got a full morning ahead." He pushed his chair noisily into the table and quickly reached for his cup to swallow down the last of his coffee. "But come in and see me anyway, when you get a minute." He smiled at her as he turned and walked out of the kitchen, and she watched him go.

If only she had known there and then that *that* was the last time they would have together. If only she had watched his departing back and had some idea what was to come, maybe there would have been something that she could have done. But of course, there wasn't, an arrhythmia could not have been predicted nor prevented. It just was, and that was it.

"Carrie. Carrie?" She continued to pound on her brother's

chest, tears rolling down her face as she sobbed for all she was worth when Dillon laid a hand on her back gently.

She continued to work on her brother, looking neither left nor right but down at his face, the face which grew ever more grey and blue, the face of a man who had died. And yet she couldn't stop, she continued to pound and plead with Joseph to open his eyes, to miraculously heal himself from within and be back there with her, back in their new life and all that they had hoped and dreamed off.

Carrie didn't know at what point Trinity had left the consulting rooms, but she was aware of her returning now with Daniel Macey at her side. She looked up into Daniel's eyes as she continued in her efforts to save her brother, and she could see the shock and devastation there.

"Carrie, he's gone." Dillon said again, gently patting her back as she continued, leaning over once again to put another breath into her brother's body. "Honey, you did your best. But he is with the Lord now," Dillon continued, and yet she carried on, unable to stop.

"Carrie." Daniel, fighting his own shock, had hurried to her and knelt down on the other side. He put an arm firmly around her shoulders, squeezing her tightly and pulling her sideways into him. "I'm so sorry, Carrie, but Joseph is dead," he said, and everything seemed suddenly so final.

"But I can't give up, I can't let him down. How can I stop now and wonder if the next minute might have helped?" Carrie felt sick and exhausted.

"Carrie, you're a doctor. You know he's gone." Daniel said gently and finally she stopped.

With her hand still leaning on her brother's chest, she bent her head forward and almost collapsed, her head on her brother's chest as she wept harder than she had ever wept in her life.

In the end, Carrie did not know how long she remained like that, she could not remember the moment at which Daniel had lifted her to her feet and then picked her up off the floor, carrying her way back into the house and away from Joseph.

CHAPTER 6

In the days which followed her brother's funeral, Carrie knew that she would soon have to occupy herself, she would have to find something to do to stop her dwelling on the sadness which threatened to overwhelm her entirely.

Everybody she knew in the town had been so kind, they had helped her almost as if the dreadful tragedy had happened out on the Oregon Trail and everybody pulled together to see what they could do to assist. In truth, she wondered if she would have been quite so surrounded by people in Missouri, even the ones who cared a good deal. Perhaps it was simply because they didn't understand in the same way. After all, most of the inhabitants of the town had travelled the Oregon Trail and had seen the tragedies and the hurried burials, the hasty goodbyes before the wagons had begun to roll again and a person's loved one was left behind in the wilderness forever.

At least Carrie had a place to visit, a headstone against which to lean flowers in the spring when winter's grip had finally released them all.

Daniel had been of particular help to her from the very moment he had arrived to see her fighting so hard to save her brother. He had helped her to arrange the funeral, had spoken to the Minister, and had organized all the supplies that Dana needed to prepare the food for mourners paying their respects.

In truth, Carrie felt as if she'd had nothing left, without Daniel she would never have managed to organize anything for herself. She couldn't even begin to think what the future might hold for her now that her beloved brother had gone. She felt as if everything had stopped in her world, everything had simply ground to a halt with a terrible bang, and nothing would ever start moving again.

"Dana tells me that you've had nothing to eat today, Carrie." Daniel appeared in the kitchen so quietly that she hadn't heard him approach. "You really do have to eat." He sat beside her at the table and reached out to lay his hand over hers.

"Everything is so strange, Daniel. Dana has been such a good girl, so caring. But I can't seem to manage anything, not even eating. Forgive me; forgive me for falling apart so dreadfully. I have seen people suffer losses and be forced to keep moving, and I know that I ought to be doing the same, but I just don't seem to be able to."

"You're doing just fine, Carrie. You'll get through this, and I'll be right here beside you. And I won't be the only one; you've got Trinity and Dillon, and Mrs. Stanton, and everybody else in this town who all care so much about you."

49

"Yes, that's very true." She said, leaning back in her chair, feeling exhausted again.

There was one person who had paid his respects who might well have kept them to himself if he had been a much more decent human being than he appeared to be. Bart Thornhill had approached her within moments of the service being completed, the moment in which she felt her grief reaching its crescendo.

"Miss Easter, I am most terribly sorry for your loss." Those were the first words that Bart Thornhill had ever spoken to her.

She had seen him before, from afar, but had never had occasion to be in conversation with the man. At the funeral, she recognized his son, Kirby, immediately. While she had never seen him before, she recognized the pale grey blue eyes as almost identical to those of Bart Thornhill. They were so alike that the two could not be mistaken as kin.

"Thank you kindly, Mr. Thornhill." Carrie had said, knowing that she ought to be gracious. Yet, at the same time, thinking that the man had no business to be at her brother's funeral.

While he was a part of the town, as much as anybody else, this was the man who had gone out of his way to silently attack her. What business did he have paying respects to a man whose sister he had tried to make trouble for? As mellow and as kind as Joseph was, he would not have been at all pleased at the idea of Bart Thornhill playing the part of a concerned fellow Townsman.

"Now, you must let me know if there's anything I can do. If there's anything you need help with, Miss Easter, you just come straight to me, do you hear?" Although the words might ordinarily have seemed kind, Carrie knew that she could not trust them.

It struck her that he was playing a role, behaving almost as some kind of town elder who had a duty to perform, a duty that he would prefer the whole town to see him carry out. And the very fact that he was using her brother's death as some sort of evidence that he was an important part of Oregon's new civilization made her silently furious.

There were so many more other people there who were genuine in their reasons for attending. Even the people who had not known Joseph particularly well had, perhaps, sought his advice as a doctor, or even noted what a pleasant man he was when they had passed in the street. It mattered not their reasons, all that mattered was that they had all truly come to pay their last respects to a good man, and that was that.

"Perhaps I *would* come to you for help, Mr. Thornhill, if you had not already gone out of your way to make trouble in my world," she said quietly, determined not to draw attention to their conversation.

Many of the mourners were looking on, probably all keen to have a moment with her to offer help also. But genuine help this time.

"Well, I would hope that you wouldn't hold that against me now. After all, I'm here to help, to do whatever I can." He spoke to her with a certain amount of authority, as if he was talking to a child.

"Then I take it that you will not interfere any further in my business?" she said coldly.

"Forgive me, young lady, but you do *not* have a business."

"Excuse me?"

"The only business you had in this town was as a part of your brother's business. Dr. Easter has sadly passed, my dear. I do not see how you can continue to operate without a real doctor."

"Mr. Thornhill, I am a doctor in all but name. I was trained by my father's hand in the same way that my brother was and I do not think it any of your business if people in this town choose to consult me. I do not have many coming to my door, Sir, but I have helped them and I will continue to do so. I do not force them to come to see me, it's by their choosing, and I would hope now, that you would leave me in peace." She shook her head from side to side as she looked at him. "If that is the only help I ever ask from you, I would hope that *that* would be enough."

"You have to understand that I have a responsibility to this town. As sorry as I feel for you and sorry as I am that a promising young man has lost his life so young, I can't just *allow* this."

"Allow it? And who are you to allow or disallow things in this town? Who do you think you are?"

"Don't raise your voice, Missy," he said, and glared at her, giving her a true picture of the man he really was.

"How dare you come here on this day of all days and demand that I keep my voice down? This is my brother's funeral, not an opportunity for you to show off to the town as if you are some kind of elder, some man of note. You are playing a role, Mr. Thornhill, and I can see right through you."

"Your hysterics will make no difference to the outcome of this. I'd already persuaded enough people to take their business to Doc Larson when your brother was still alive. People who might ordinarily have been persuaded to put their lives and their health in the hands of a woman who calls herself a doctor. Well, we're just not going to have that sort of thing in our town, and you'd better get used to it."

"And you'd better take your talk elsewhere, Thornhill." Suddenly, Daniel was at her side. "Before I tell the whole town exactly what it is you're saying to a grieving woman at her brother's graveside. Clear out." Daniel took a step towards Bart Thornhill.

"You'll regret your interference, Macey. You might think that you're in with a chance in the provisional government, but I'll see to it that the door gets slammed in your face. You will regret this, you see if you don't."

"Neither one of us has a part in the provisional government, Thornhill, so I don't see how you get to slam doors just yet. Either way, this is not the time or the place. Miss Easter is grieving and you are making things worse." Daniel began to speak at a more obvious tone, and it was clear that some of the other mourners were beginning to pay closer attention.

Seeing that there was no way for him to continue, Bart Thornhill nodded his head graciously at Carrie before turning to take his leave, his son glaring at Daniel all the while.

Daniel had taken her side and had continued to care for her closely. Not a day went by when she did not see him, and he had more than once taken her into his strong arms and held her tightly as she wept, her grief refusing to release its hold on her.

As she had drifted off into reverie, she had not noticed how Daniel had risen and cut a small piece of bread, buttering it before setting it down on a plate in front of her.

"Joseph would want you to get through this, Carrie. Joseph would want you to carry on, as if you were out there now on the wagon train moving forward; forward day by day. But you have to look after yourself to be able to do it, you have to eat." He reached out and gently stroked her cheek, his bright blue eyes staring into hers with the greatest concern.

"Thank you, Daniel. I don't know how I would survive this without you," Carrie said, and finally picked up the bread-and-butter and began to eat.

CHAPTER 7

*S*everal weeks after Joseph's death, Carrie had found herself reorganizing the small infirmary. She wasn't even sure why she was bothering without Joseph, except to think that she probably just needed something to do. Her patients had dwindled to almost nothing, and certainly everybody who had been Joseph's patient had not returned.

What had been most surprising and most upsetting of all was the number of ladies who had once trusted her opinion, trusted her enough to see her and her alone, who had not returned to her after her brother's death.

As Carrie tucked in the pristine sheets around the beds she had pointlessly redressed, she heard the door into the main office open, and close. It took her by surprise and she wondered who on earth had decided to make their way to the doctor's practice which had no doctor.

She hurried out into the waiting area to see Daniel smiling

broadly. At his side stood Mrs. Stanton, a kindly smile on her face, her eyes full of concern.

"What a nice surprise to see you both here," Carrie said, feeling suddenly pleased to have some company.

For weeks, she had been unable to function in ordinary conversation, and had been dreading visitors, even from those who cared about her the most. Today, for some reason, perhaps it was the different setting, somewhere other than the kitchen table where she had done most of her grieving, she felt a little better.

"I know you're still suffering, Doc, but I wondered when you'd be up and running again." Mrs. Stanton began cautiously. "I mean, I wouldn't mind a little more of that black cohosh and a quick check over." She smiled and held out the empty glass jar, her pink cheeks testament to the fact that she had been some days without her treatment.

"Really? I mean, you'd still come here to see me? Even though Joseph is…" She couldn't finish.

"I sure did like your brother, Doc, but it was always you I came here to see. Me, and some of the ladies have been talking about it and we didn't like to just drop in on you with all our problems again as if nothing had changed. We all know you've been suffering, we all know you're still grieving. And to be straight with you, Doc, we miss you."

"Mrs. Stanton, I cannot tell you what that means to me." And suddenly, Carrie was in floods of tears.

This time, however, they were actually tears of joy, tears of relief that she had not, perhaps, lost everything.

"Oh, now you come here, honey." Mrs. Stanton crossed the room in no time and pulled Carrie into her arms, hugging her tightly against her robust frame. "Surely you didn't think we'd abandon the only doc who listens to us old girls." She laughed and it was a wonderful, comforting sound, a sound with a life of its own that Carrie could feel reverberating around the older woman's chest.

"Right, well you just come on through with me to the consulting room, Mrs. Stanton," Carrie said, straightening up and hurriedly drying her eyes, smiling and trying to appear professional. "We can't have you going without your black cohosh, can we? And I have something else for you to try as well, something which might go some way to easing your other symptoms."

"Well, let's get to it, and I'm happy for you to call me Jeanne, Doc," Mrs. Stanton said and looked back at Daniel. "You're to stay here, young man. You don't need to hear what it is us ladies are going to talk about."

Daniel stifled a laugh and caught Carrie's eye before she followed the older woman, who was already making her way into the consulting room. He looked amused and caring all at once and Carrie felt, in that moment, that she had most certainly turned a corner. She felt better, not mended entirely, but there was now hope of it.

Jeannie Stanton had made herself comfortable in the consulting room for almost half an hour, going over all her symptoms again, and listening patiently as Carrie explained to her how best to use the evening primrose oil that she had given her to take alongside her black cohosh.

By the time Jeannie left, with a promise that she would let all the other ladies know that the *doc* was ready to start seeing them again, Carrie wondered if Daniel might have already left. After all, he would have been sitting there for some time.

However, as she showed out a very much happier, Mrs. Jeanne Stanton, Carrie was pleased to see that Daniel was still waiting patiently, still smiling as he hurriedly opened the door for the older woman.

"You're a gentleman, Daniel Macey," she said as she bustled away and he closed the door, laughing.

"Yes, you really are a gentleman, Daniel Macey." Carrie took a step towards him. "And don't think I don't realize that you talked Mrs. Stanton into coming back." She grinned at him.

"I just asked how she was, that's all." Daniel began, but his grin said otherwise. "Well, I did mention that you would certainly welcome a visit, especially if Mrs. Stanton needed help of any kind, or even... would be so kind as to help...."

"And the minute she agreed, you wasted no time in getting her here, walking her here yourself, to make sure that she did come." Despite her words, Carrie was smiling broadly. "And I can't thank you enough, Daniel, really I can't. It makes me feel as if I have a purpose again, even if I never have a full and busy practice, just a few of the ladies will be enough to make me feel as if I am still doing my job."

"And don't forget, sooner or later that wagon train is going to pull into this town again. Just a few months from now, there will be more ladies here than old Doc Larson can cope with. He'll be begging you to take them off his hands." Daniel laughed, a laugh which turned into a cough.

"Are you alright, Daniel?" Carrie said, eyeing him curiously.

"Yeah, I'm actually fine." He smiled and cleared his throat.

"I don't know, you've cleared your throat a fair bit these last few days. Here, let me take a look." She advanced upon him.

"You doctors, you're always looking for sickness," he said and smiled, taking a step back from her and holding his hands up as if to fend her off. "I've just got a tickle in my throat, that's all." He grinned and she laughed at his comical, dramatic display.

"Well, suffer on if you will, but I could have helped," she said and smiled.

"Actually, I think there is a way you can help my sore throat." He said, and stared at her intently for a moment.

Carrie felt her heart beat just a little quicker as he took a step towards her and reached out, placing a hand on either side of her face. She knew he was going to kiss her and already she felt so many different emotions she could hardly count them. She was afraid, almost terrified, and yet, at the same time, she could hardly wait to feel his lips on hers.

And when they finally arrived, when he finally kissed her, Carrie knew she had never felt such a wonderful sensation in her entire life. She kissed him back with a passion that she hardly knew she possessed.

CHAPTER 8

"*O*h, Carrie, I thought things were suddenly taking a turn for the better. And you and Daniel, after the kiss and everything." Trinity let out a great puff of air. "It seemed so perfect."

"Do you remember when I said I thought he might be too good to be true?" Carrie said a little bitterly.

"Look, maybe it's just a mistake, maybe you should talk about it?" Trinity said and leaned her elbows heavily on the kitchen table. "He probably already realizes what he's done and I guess he would be real sorry to know how much it hurt your feelings."

"It's more than just hurting my feelings, Trinity." Carrie sighed. "He knows what it meant to me to have a father and a brother who believed in me completely. And you know what, I thought he really believed in me too. I thought that Daniel Macey had faith in my ability. That day when he brought Jeannie Stanton into see me, when he said that he was sure that other ladies would follow again, I just assumed that he thought I was a good doctor. It more than hurt."

"I guess he let you down real bad, huh?" Trinity said, clearly not seeing the sense in continuing to claim Daniel's behavior as a simple mistake, albeit a thoughtless one.

"I've never felt so let down in my life. And I know he's been so good to me, Trinity; he's been so kind and caring and even protective, but I can hardly look at him."

"Are you absolutely sure that Daniel wasn't already Dr. Larson's patient?" Trinity asked, looking hopeful as she alighted upon a fresh idea.

"No, Joseph had already told me that Daniel was his patient. He looked after his health on the way over the Oregon Trail and Daniel was one of his first official patients here in Oregon. No, to my knowledge, this is the first time that he has consulted Dr. Larson."

"I see." Trinity had an air of defeat about her, as if there was nothing left for her to say.

"And believe me, I have absolutely nothing against Dr. Larson. From everything I've heard, he's a fine physician, just as my brother was."

"I'm sure that's true, but at the same time, I can't help but wonder if he has some ties to Bart Thornhill. That man is pure spite from head to toe, really he is. As nice as Dr. Larson is, he must know that Bart Thornhill has done whatever he can to convince your patients to go to him."

"Maybe he does and maybe he doesn't, Trinity, I just don't know. What I do know is that Daniel *chose* to go to him. Daniel chose to go to his offices and ask for his opinion on his throat."

"You don't know for sure that it was his throat, Carrie. After all, it might have been something a little more personal, something that he didn't want to say to you. After all, the two of you have been getting closer and closer and he might just have been embarrassed."

"I know I can't be sure, and yet at the same time, I know it. I could tell by the look on his face when the two of us almost bumped into each other outside Dr. Larson's surgery. I never saw a man more guilty in all my life."

Carrie sighed and rested her own elbows on the table, leaning her chin heavily in her hands. Daniel really had looked guilty as he had hurried out of Dr. Larson's office with the small bottle in his hand. Carrie hadn't seen exactly what it was, but looking back she guessed it was some kind of anti-septic to cure whatever infection was laying in his throat.

The moment she realized what was happening, Carrie found that she was unable to speak. They were standing just a foot apart and looking at each other, Carrie unable to take her eyes from his. She knew that her mouth hung open just a little and it was likely *that* which showed him exactly how shocked and disappointed she really was.

"Carrie, really, it's nothing serious." He said and smiled, already trying to make light of it.

"Yes, so you said when you refused to let *me* take a look at you," she said coldly.

"Carrie, please," he said, his voice low and yet beseeching.

"Please what?" She asked, gathering herself and folding her arms defensively across her chest.

It had been just two days since he'd kissed her and she could hardly believe that the man she had been daydreaming about ever since would have done something so hurtful.

"I haven't come here to upset you. It's near my office and I......"

"Don't bother." Carrie said and held a hand up to silence him. "In the end, the physician you choose to trust is your affair and nobody else's. It's certainly none of my business, it's nothing to me." Carrie turned on her heel to head back in the opposite direction.

In truth, she was so angry that she could hardly remember what she was heading into town for in the first place. It mattered not, because she knew she could not contain the angry tears which threatened to fall. Whatever she had needed in town would have to wait.

"Carrie, don't go," he said and made to reach for her, but she was too quick for him.

Carrie didn't wait a moment longer, nor did she turn to see if he was following her. She walked as quickly as she could, desperate to get back to the safety and privacy of her home.

Trinity reached out and laid a hand on her shoulder, bringing her back into the present.

"I still think you should talk to him," Trinity said cautiously. "I'm sure he'll come around sooner or later wanting to speak."

"He already has," Carrie said and shrugged.

"He did? Well, what did he say?"

"I didn't wait around long enough to speak to him. I saw him striding up the road, looking at me, and I knew he was heading for the house. I knew he was coming to see me, but I just didn't want to hear it. All I could think of was how I had offered to help him and he had simply kissed me so that he didn't have to have me treat him. For all he defended me in front of Bart Thornhill, Daniel doesn't think I'm any more capable than *that* awful man does."

"And so, you walked away?"

"I did, I turned my back on him and walked into the house and slammed the door," Carrie said dolefully.

"However you feel about Daniel now, trust me, he is nothing like Bart Thornhill. That man is wicked, he is so intent on owning everything and having everything his way that he would do anything. Surely, you don't think that Daniel Macey is anything like that?"

"No, I don't think that. But he has no faith in me, not the sort of faith that I would expect from somebody who kisses me."

"I still think that Bart Thornhill has a lot to answer for," Trinity said, intent upon flogging a dead horse. "He's already interfering in Dillon's building work. Do you know, one of the suppliers of the timber for the merchant store has already told Dillon, that Kirby Thornhill tried to pay him off, tried to get him to either not supply the wood for the building at all, or to supply poor quality wood. And I can't tell if he's angry that Dillon married me instead of him, or if it's because we're building a merchant store, and the Thornhill's didn't think to do it first. They're so dangerous, and they're getting more and more powerful." Trinity paused. "Just consider at least keeping Daniel as a friend. He is a good man deep down, and he's a good attorney. Just think about it."

"I'll try," Carrie said without conviction.

"And don't you go thinking that he only kissed you to stop you inspecting that throat of his. I've seen the way he looks at you, and I've seen that look of attraction grow into a look of love over the months. I'm sure he's fallen in love with you, Carrie, I really am. And we're all allowed one mistake, aren't we?"

"Maybe."

CHAPTER 9

*D*aniel hadn't worked for two days straight. Since he had yet to either employ an assistant or partner up with another attorney, he'd had to close his offices and hope for the best.

However, as much as he wanted to keep going, he hadn't felt so unwell for as long as he could remember. It had progressed far beyond a sore, tight throat, and he knew that Doc Larson's tonic wasn't doing anything to make him feel better.

"It sounds like a throat infection at this stage, Daniel, but I want you to come right back here in two days if you don't see any signs of progress after taking this." He'd pushed a bottle of dark colored liquid across the table at him. "Just a spoonful three times a day." He said with a nod.

"Sure thing, Doc." Daniel smiled and took the bottle.

Daniel thought back and realized, he was never really a man who had spent much time in a physician's office. Never actually consulted Joseph more than once since they had arrived in Oregon. Joseph dealt with a malady or two when they had been part of the wagon train, but it was only to be expected. Everybody was exhausted, and illness took hold so much more easily on a tired body.

In truth, he liked Doc Larson well enough, but was pleased with the idea that he would probably see him very rarely. He wasn't really sure why he hadn't let Carrie take a look at him. After all, it was a simple sore throat, or at least *that* was what he had thought at the time.

It wasn't until he came face-to-face with Carrie outside Doc Larson's office, and seen the look which told him without a doubt that he had let her down. He thought of it in a little more depth. In truth, he thought he hadn't let her look at him in case she couldn't solve it. If it was something that couldn't be treated, or was too simple to be treated and would go on its own, he didn't want her to have to say it to him.

Of course, now, he realized that *that* was exactly the same thing as having no faith in her person. He had already pre-empted her failure without giving her an opportunity to prove herself. And she did not need to *prove* herself, to him of all people, surely.

Daniel let out a great sigh and realized there was effort in it. His throat seemed tighter than ever, almost as if there was something tied about it. He reached out instinctively and ran his fingers down the front, half expecting to find a great protrusion. Yet there was nothing, nothing at all to explain why it was that he was finding it increasingly difficult to simply breathe.

Daniel settled himself down in a chair by the fire that had exhausted him when he had fought to get it alight. It was a cold winter's day and he felt chilled to the very bone, much colder than he thought he would feel had he been in better health.

After two days of taking the remedy that Doc Larson had given him, Daniel knew that it was not working. He didn't blame the doc, of course, because he had told him to return if the remedy made no difference. And yet he couldn't, he couldn't do that to Carrie.

Instead, he'd made his way across town to her house, hoping that she would at least see him. It had only been two days and yet he found he'd missed her terribly. Even before her brother had died, he'd seen her regularly, but since his dear friend had passed, Daniel had seen Carrie every day without fail.

If only his old friend were still there, if only Joseph hadn't died. He couldn't begin to explain, not even to Carrie, how much he missed him. The two of them had become as brothers on the Oregon Trail. Its trials and hardships had cemented a friendship which ought to have lasted a lifetime. When that friendship had been cut short, Daniel had felt one less connection to the world, and it had upset him dreadfully.

And then there was Carrie. She was still alive, and yet he missed her just as much. If only he had not been so thoughtless, if only he had not pushed her away from him with the only slight that could truly cut her to her very heart. If only he had trusted her.

Daniel knew that he had loved her from the very first day he met her. Joseph talked of his sister much on their long days of walking and struggling with the wagon train. Without even meeting her, Daniel had already formed a great interest in a woman so intelligent, that her brother described her as every bit the doctor he was.

And then, when he had first set eyes on her, his enchantment was complete. She had spoken brightly and with intelligence, and there seemed already to be that link which bound the people who had made that terrible journey, and probably always would. And of course, when he'd seen her cheeks flush a little as they'd made eye contact, he immediately hoped that she was as attracted to him as he was to her.

Things had progressed nicely, and he had felt them moving towards each other bit by bit even before Joseph had died. And afterwards, of course, they had grown closer still, both of them tortured by the grief of such a shocking and sudden loss.

Daniel could feel his heart beating just a little harder and realized that he was finding it more and more difficult to breathe. Suddenly, he wanted to get away from the warmth of the fire, feeling that the warm air was somehow making things harder. He rose to his feet and tried once again to take in a good breath. However, it seemed as if something was squeezing his windpipe, something that would not allow more than a hiss of breath through. He was beginning to panic, but he knew that that was making things worse. The more he panicked, the harder he tried to draw breath into his lungs and the more he was horrified to find that he could not.

In the end, he knew he needed the cold outdoor air, he needed a doctor. Without even stopping to put on his coat, Daniel stumbled to the door of his house and pulled it open, almost falling out of it into the road. Managing to stay on his feet, and leaving his door wide open behind him, Daniel decided to take the longer route to help, the route that would take him directly to Carrie.

CHAPTER 10

*F*or a whole day and a night Carrie had thought about everything that Trinity had said. In truth, she knew that Daniel really was a good man, a kind man who had helped her through the worst of times. She could hardly think of another person in the world that she felt as close to as she did to Daniel, and she thought that it was perhaps *that* which had made his betrayal of her so difficult to bear.

There was now no man in the world who truly believed in her as her father and brother had. To discover that Daniel did not believe in her, had made her feel suddenly very alone, as if there would truly be little point in ever going to Boston or Pennsylvania even if that opportunity one day, miraculously, arose.

With no patients that day, Carrie had made her way back into the house and sat at the kitchen table nursing a strong cup of coffee. Suddenly, the peace was shattered when she heard the sounds of shouting outside in the road. Dana had rushed past her to see what was happening and turned to her with a look of horror.

"It's Daniel Macey, Carrie," she said in a high-pitched squeak. "Dillon Goodman is helping him, holding him up, I think they're trying to get in to the consulting room."

With a sinking feeling and a racing heart, Carrie got to her feet and charged through the house and out to the men. Dillon and Daniel were leaning in an ungainly, curious fashion against the door as Dillon tried to open it.

"Here, let me." Carrie opened the door and helped to get Daniel inside.

Daniel's face was grey, his lips tinged with blue, and she had a sudden, awful memory of her brother laying on the floor of his consulting room.

But Daniel was alive, he was upright and his eyes were open. He was pointing at his neck trying to breathe, his eyes bulging.

"Sit him here." Carrie insisted, and pulled out a chair so that Dillon could gently push Daniel down into it. "Just nod or shake your head, Daniel." She began and dropped to her knees in front of him, staring into his face. "Is there something in your throat?" She looked at him and he nodded. "Is it something that you were eating, something that you put into your mouth?" He shook his head from side to side and made a squeezing motion of his throat and then shrugged helplessly.

"Daniel, do you feel as if your throat is swelling up without reason, that you can't get your breath?" She went on, struggling to control her shaking hands.

When Daniel nodded vigorously, she realized that his throat infection, if that was what it was, had taken a very drastic turn.

Suddenly and without warning, the door opened again and there stood Bart Thornhill. He had a furious look on his face and Carrie could see that, standing just behind him, was his son, Kirby.

"I saw Goodman bringing Daniel Macey here. Is he unwell?"

"Yes, he is, can you please leave." Carrie said with determination. She knew that it was no time to be arguing with the man who had made himself her enemy.

"Well, if he is ill, he needs a doctor," Bart snarled.

"And he's got one." Dillon Goodman said, dependable as always.

"Kirby, run down and get Dr. Larson now. Tell him what's happening and don't come back here without him." Bart Thornhill barked at his son who hurriedly ran off to do his father's bidding.

"I'm going to put a stop to this, Missy. If anything happens to that man, I'll find some way to see that charges are brought down on you." As Bart spoke, Daniel became more and more distressed.

He tried to turn in his seat to look at Bart, but his breathing was growing more and more labored.

"Daniel, please just ignore him." Carrie said hurriedly. As she looked into his face, Daniel's eyes suddenly flew wide open and she knew in that awful moment that breathing had suddenly become impossible for him.

He writhed in his seat, clawing at his throat, a desperate look on his face as he tried to draw in just an ounce of life-giving air. His face was growing darker and darker and she knew that she would have to act quickly or he would die right in front of her, just as her brother had.

"Dillon, help me get him to the floor," she said, and Dillon immediately helped lay him out.

"Don't you dare help her. She doesn't know what she's doing, she couldn't even save her own brother, for God's sake." Bart was almost shouting.

In a heartbeat, Dillon Goodman was on his feet standing toe to toe with the man who thought himself the most powerful in Oregon.

"Dillon, there isn't time. Please, run into the infirmary and bring me some cloth, alcohol, and a scalpel. Oh yes, and a dropper bottle.

"Which sort?" Dillon said, already making his way.

"Any, it doesn't matter."

Dillon returned in no time and Carrie was relieved to see that he had everything that she had asked him for. Despite Bart Thornhill's voluble protestations, Carrie hastily cleaned Daniel's throat with alcohol and looked on with dismay as his eyes began to close. His body was growing limp, and she knew she didn't have a moment to spare.

Just as she had lifted the scalpel to his throat, her hand entirely steady, not shaking as she assumed it would be, there was a great clattering at the door as Kirby Thornhill returned with Dr. Larson.

"For God's sake, do something, Larson. This woman is about to cut his throat," Bart said angrily.

"No, she isn't, she is about to save his life. Step aside, you fool," Dr. Larson said and moved into the room just as Carrie made a deep incision.

Without a word, Dr. Larson removed the glass tube from the dropper bottle and snapped off the thin end. He handed it to her and she carefully inserted the smooth, uncut end into the incision she had made in Daniel's windpipe.

The very moment it was in place, there was a great wheezing sound and Daniel's chest rose high. Silence fell in the room as even Bart Thornhill watched with amazement. Carrie blinked back tears of emotion as she saw Daniel's chest begin to rise and fall rhythmically. Her emergency treatment had worked and she knew then that she had saved his life. All that remained now was to figure out how to reduce the inflammation in his throat.

"What's happening?" Bart Thornhill barked as if it was his right.

"I'll tell you what's happening, Bart Thornhill." Dr. Larson rose to his feet and glared at him. "You have just witnessed a very fine doctor saving a man's life. His throat is blocked, likely infected, and she very quickly realized that he would die if she didn't find some other means to get air into his lungs. She has bypassed that part of his windpipe altogether, hence the scalpel and the tube. Do you have any more pointless questions? If not, it's probably time for you to leave."

Despite having a patient on the floor, Carrie couldn't help but look on in wonder. She had never spoken to Dr. Larson before, and realized now that she had wrongly assumed him to be her enemy. She looked up at him gratefully.

"I believe you have a small infirmary, Miss Easter," Dr.

Larson said as he watched Bart Thornhill and his son take their leave.

"Yes, it's just through here" she indicated with a nod of her head.

"Well, perhaps Mr. Goodman and I can carry Daniel through to one of the beds." He looked at Dillon who nodded vigorously. "And then perhaps you might allow me to assist you to see what can be done for this infection. I must admit, he did come to see me and I did prescribe an anti-bacterial tonic, but it obviously has not worked."

"Don't go blaming yourself, Dr. Larson. I think I know why Daniel didn't come back to see you when it wasn't working," she said and looked at his sorrowful face.

"Well, let's get him well right now, shall we?" Dr. Larson knelt beside her and smiled. Suddenly, an overwhelming feeling of reassurance washed over her.

CHAPTER 11

"*He* certainly looks a lot better. Has he woken up at all overnight?" Dr. Larson reappeared in the infirmary the following day.

He had managed to get a good look down Daniel's throat and had even been able to lance the great poisonous lump which had developed inside.

The two of them had worked together and Carrie had been pleased to see a procedure that she had never seen before. Dr. Larson had talked her through it, just as her father used to do when he was treating somebody, and she had felt herself strangely growing in confidence again. Dr. Larson had spoken to her as a contemporary, not as the silly, interfering woman that Bart Thornhill had assumed her to be.

"That wound is healing already." He looked down at the place from where the tube had previously protruded.

As soon as the poison had been lanced, Daniel had already begun to attempt to breathe normally. Unfortunately, he had swallowed a good deal of the poison and it had made him a little sick during the night.

"He's had something of a rough night, Dr. Larson, but his color's returning now and his temperature has come down a good deal. I think it's just a case of time now." She smiled at him broadly. "And thank you for everything."

"Not at all, there wasn't a moment to waste and if you hadn't acted as quickly as you had, this young man wouldn't be here now." Dr. Larson paused for a moment, clearly having something to say and wondering quite how he would say it. "I wonder if you might like to work with me, Miss Easter." He began a little cautiously.

"Work with you?" she said, somewhat surprised.

"Not as an assistant, you understand," he said hurriedly, as if he feared insulting her. "Something more than that, really. I was thinking that your establishment here is a very good one. I certainly don't have enough beds in my practice, and wonder if we could make use of both my office and yours."

"I think that's a wonderful idea. But I only have a few patients, Sir."

"Then we will work it between us and see what happens." He smiled. "And I've heard good things from back East of late. I think you might find that the day that young ladies are accepted into medical colleges is soon coming. But until that time comes, I should very much appreciate the help."

"Well, thank you for your consideration." She smiled, feeling suddenly a part of something bigger.

"Well, you just think on it and let me have your answer. In the meantime, well done, you saved this man's life." Dr.

Larson smiled at her before nodding graciously and turning to make his way out of the infirmary.

Feeling somewhat surprised, albeit pleasantly so, Carrie sat down in the chair next to Daniel's bed. She could hardly believe the offer, and she only wished that she could see the look on Bart Thornhill's face when all was discovered. In fact, the very idea of it made her chuckle.

"What's so funny?" Daniel croaked, speaking for the first time since he had arrived desperate and unable to breathe the day before.

"You're awake? How do you feel?"

"Kind of rough," he said, and gave her a lopsided grin. "Kind of sick and sore and a little bit like my body doesn't belong to me anymore." He chuckled, but it looked painful. "But nowhere near as bad as I felt when I thought you'd never speak to me again."

"Look, Daniel, you don't really need to think about that now. You just need to concentrate on getting better, alright?" Carrie said, not keen to be reminded how his thoughtlessness has made her feel.

"Please forgive me, I should have trusted you."

"Well, I suppose you're not the first man to assume I don't know what I'm doing. And I daresay you won't be the last." She looked at him sadly.

"But now I know for sure, and I was a fool not to know it in the first place." He tried to clear his throat and Carrie quickly pulled a pillow from one of the other beds and held him up so that she could place it behind his head.

"It might be better if you didn't try to talk for a while," she said gently.

"No, I have to. I have things I need to say to you, Doc, and I'm not going to get any rest until I've said them."

"*Doc*, huh?" she said with a laugh.

"Carrie, you're every bit the doctor that your brother told me you were. Now please, let a man make just one mistake in his life and forgive him for it." He smiled hopefully. "And then, when you've forgiven him, for God's sake, agree to marry him."

"Are you proposing to me, Daniel Macey?"

"I am proposing to you, Carrie. I love you, and not just because you saved my life. I've loved you for a long time and I know I made a mistake, but I swear to you I will never make another one."

"That's kind of a hefty promise to make for anybody, even me. People make mistakes, Daniel, and I do forgive you," she said as tears welled in her eyes. "And I love you, but if you can't come to terms with who I am, with what I want to do with my life, I can't marry you."

"I swear to you I won't get in the way. Even Dr. Larson thinks that Boston or Pennsylvania will come good soon, I heard him say so. You'll get your place there, and when you do, I'll be right by your side."

"Do you really mean that?"

"I sure do. I won't make the mistake of losing you again, Carrie. These last few days have been hell for me. Not just because my throat was swelling up and I knew I was in trouble. I realized that I just can't bear not to see you every day, not to hear your voice and see that beautiful smile. So yes, I'll follow you to Boston or Pennsylvania, whatever happens, and then we'll come back here and you can carry on in the practice that your brother wanted you to work in. What do you say? For God's sake, will you put a sick man out of his misery?" He grinned.

"Just so long as you know that if you do try to get in my way, I'll go without you," Carrie said with her hands on her hips.

"I have no doubt, and I dare not try and stop you," Daniel laughed painfully.

"And of course, I'll marry you, Daniel. I love you so much." She pulled her chair up tight against his bed and leaned over, laying her head gently on his chest. "When I thought I was going to lose you, I didn't think I could carry on in this world. And you're right, we all make mistakes."

"I really love you, Carrie."

"And I love you, Daniel." As her head lay on his chest and she looked up into his eyes, the sound of his heart beating was the most wonderful sound in the world.

* * *

To FIND out when our next book is available join our exclusive newsletter and receive 2 FREE books http://amzn.to/2shQ9Ym

PREVIEW OF OUR NEXT BOOK
JOSIE'S STORY

Please forgive me for any errors as this book is still in the final stages of editing but I thought you might like to get an exclusive look at it.

John Shepherd stretched his arms high above his head in an attempt to relieve the ache in his overworked shoulders. He'd put in a long day, just as he did every day, constantly moving to stave off the chill of the cool early spring air. But not only that, John was keen to stick to the promise that he had made to the kind Townswomen of Oregon.

John was perfectly well aware how much he had to be grateful for, even in the midst of all his own sadness. Jeannie Stanton and a full complement of other ladies had been arranged as carers for his baby by Trinity Goodman and Carrie Easter. They had never once let him down and he was determined to return the favour.

Every morning, just as the sun was coming up, Jeannie arrived to take the first shift, always striding in bright and happy, not a yawn nor a stretch in sight. She was a fine woman who seemed to adore baby Suki and John could not help but think that she liked the early morning shift so that she could feed his daughter and get her washed and dressed in something pretty.

Ever since Trinity had set about helping him and enlisting the help of others, John had been inundated with clothes for his daughter, far more than he and Leonora would ever have been able to afford themselves.

As always, thoughts of Leonora seemed to stop him in his tracks. John had been slowly coming to terms with the worst of all losses and yet still his loss had the ability to almost floor him. Sighing deeply, he crossed the single room which had been home to him and his baby daughter since they had arrived just six months before from the arduous deprivations of the Oregon Trail. He peered down into the little crib and smiled when he saw Suki was still fast asleep, just as she had been when he had arrived back at their meagre little home after a long day's work.

Jeannie had spent the entire day with Suki, as she always did on a Tuesday, and she had left him a warm stew on the stove. Hardly a day went by when one of the ladies did not leave him something to tuck into when he came in from his farmlands and he was always relieved and humbled by it. If he lived to be one hundred years old, John did not know how he would repay the Townswomen for their unerring kindness.

"John?"

He recognised Trinity's voice immediately; she always called out and then tapped on the door.

"Trinity, come in." John hurriedly open the door and pulled it wide. "Suki is fast asleep," he said with a smile.

"She sure is a good sleeper, John. I reckon you have been real lucky with her, she is a good little baby." Trinity smiled at him before darting across the room to peer down into the crib just as he had done moments before.

"I reckon she's asleep more than she's awake." John laughed. "But I will wake her gently in a little while and feed her before she goes down for the night. She is not just a sleepy baby, she is a real hungry one too."

"Well, I won't keep you, I can see you haven't eaten yet." She eyed the pan on the tiny stove. "I just wanted to see how long you reckon it will be before you move into your farmhouse. I might have some news for you."

"Oh, I see. Well, I reckon it won't be more than a couple weeks now. Dillon's help sure did make a difference and I'm much further on than I thought I'd be. It's just a few finishing touches now and a bit of furniture and me an Suki will be settling in." He smiled broadly, warmed as he always was by the thought of moving his baby girl out of the one-room lodgings they had been in for four months and into the home that he had been building.

John wondered what he would have done without Trinity and Dillon since he'd arrived in Oregon. Where Trinity had helped him with the care of his baby, Dillon had been equally helpful with the building of his farmhouse.

Fresh from his win of the bucking bronco competition purse, Dillon had begun to build his merchant store almost immediately. He'd been able to pay several of the locals to help him out and, more than once, had sent them over for the day to help John get along with his own building. It was the sort of help that was invaluable and had moved things on for John very quickly. Without that sort of help, it would have been several more weeks before he could have reached the stage he was at.

"I bet you can't wait," Trinity said with a smile as she looked about the little room.

"You have that right, Trinity." He also gave a laugh. "I reckon this room gets smaller and smaller by the day."

"You've done so well to get so far so quickly." Trinity stared off into the middle distance. "Not only is your house all but ready, but Dillon tells me that you've already ploughed up a couple of your fields and started growing. It won't be long before you're ready to start selling, will it?"

"In a few weeks, I'll be selling the first of the root vegetables, then the beans and what not. And I turned a whole field over to wheat, so that should give me more income later in the summer." John smiled, proud of his achievements and excited by the thought that he would soon be selling.

"That's real good, John. And there isn't a person in town who could say you haven't worked for it, honey, because you sure have."

"Thanks, Trinity. It means a lot, but I couldn't have done it without all the help. I mean you, Dr Carrie, not to mention Jeannie Stanton and Dillon. I was just thinking before you came this evening that I have no clue how I'll ever repay such kindness."

"You don't need to repay, John. It's enough for all of us to see you get on and it's not as if we haven't all received a little kindness along the way ourselves. I mean, if it hadn't been for Dillon and Carrie, me and Ma would never have got here, we would have just been stranded. And I'm sure that it's a tale that could be told again and again from just that one year on the Oregon Trail. And no doubt it will be told again and again come September or October when the next load arrives from Missouri."

"I guess so, but I'm still so grateful." He smiled. "Anyway, what's your news? You said you might have some news for me?"

"Oh yes, I was thinking about you today when I saw Josie Lane, do you know her?" Trinity raised her eyebrows expectantly.

"I can't say I do, but I guess I spend so much of my time out on the farm that the only people I see are you and Dillon and the ladies who come to look after Suki."

"Sure, of course," Trinity said and nodded. "Well, Josie Lane came across the Oregon Trail a year before we did. She is only young, just seventeen now, and she lost both of her parents along the way."

"That's real tough, did she have any other family with her?" John said, feeling the familiar pain of loss in the middle of his chest.

"No, it was just the three of them. The problem for Josie was that she didn't have any family back in Missouri either, no family at all."

"So, she just kept going?"

"There was nothing else for it. She was so far along the trail she would never have made it back by herself. But a family took her in, the Armstrongs."

"I can't say I've heard of them either."

"Well, they're setting up a farm just as you are, although they're getting on very nicely since they have not only their own equipment they brought with them, but they drove Josie's family wagon the rest of the way also."

"So, Josie's family were going to set up a farm themselves, were they?"

"Yes, but Josie couldn't carry on alone. She was barely sixteen when she arrived in Oregon and the Armstrongs took her in. She's been keeping house for them, since they had money enough to get their place built in no time at all, and she also takes in laundry from the single men of the town and some of the better off families."

"She sounds like a hard worker. Poor kid," John said sadly.

"She is a hard worker, perhaps a little too hard." Trinity paused for a moment and chewed her bottom lip. "The thing is, she almost works for nothing."

"What do you mean?"

"She keeps house for the Armstrongs and does little bits and pieces about the farm. But her laundry money, every penny of it, she has to pay to the Armstrongs also. They say it is for her keep, her bed and board."

"But surely keeping house, cooking and cleaning I daresay, and little jobs about the farm would be enough for bed and board, wouldn't it?" John found himself distracted for the first time in a long time, as if there was some comfort in applying his sympathies to the problems of somebody other than himself.

"To be honest, that is exactly what I thought. She takes in a lot of laundry, she is working from morning till night. I just can't help thinking that she's trapped there. Unable to save or make any sort of life herself because every penny she earns goes to the Armstrongs." Trinity peered down into the crib once more as baby Suki began to stir. "I sure don't want to say anything bad about the Armstrongs because they got her here to Oregon and they're looking after her in their own way."

"Well, you can leave it to *me* to say something bad about them," John said, feeling somewhat annoyed for the young girl on her behalf. "Because they are taking advantage, no doubts of that."

"I'm glad you said it." Trinity smiled.

"It's one thing to take somebody in and help them and something else altogether if you're doing it to line your pockets. It sounds to me as if they've turned her into some kind of household servant without any rights or means to make a life for herself. If they take all her money, every penny she earns, then she can't make any choices, unless somebody marries her. And that kind of a marriage for a girl of just seventeen is no good, is it?"

John thought back to his own wedding, himself marrying at seventeen. But that was very different, he'd met Leonora when they were both sixteen and they were so in love that there was no thought of them making a mistake. Even as he'd walked up the aisle, John had no doubts, no regrets. And he knew that Leonora felt the same.

And when she had become pregnant with their first child when they were both just eighteen, John knew that their world was complete. He'd never once considered how his happiness could turn to sorrow. He'd never assumed for one moment when his beloved wife had become pregnant that he would be raising their child alone.

"Well, she could end up just as trapped, couldn't she? A young girl like that who needs a marriage to save her can tend to attract the wrong kind of man." Trinity nodded. "But let's not marry her off just yet." She laughed.

"You have a plan of some sort Trinity, I can see in your face." John raised his eyebrows, Trinity always had a plan.

"Well, I was just thinking that in a few weeks' time you might well be in a position to take Josie on to care for Suki."

Is had always been John's plan to only rely on the kindness of the women of the town for as long as he absolutely needed to. He'd told them all from the very beginning that as soon as he had his house built and his farm up and running that he would employ a housekeeper, someone to live in who would look after Suki whilst he was out at work. Perhaps by taking on Josie he would be solving both of their problems.

"I think that sounds like a fine idea, Trinity. Why don't you speak to her about it and see what the young woman thinks about moving away from the Armstrongs?"

"I sure was hoping you were going to say that," Trinity said with a knowing smile.

* * *

To find out when our Josie's Story is available join our exclusive newsletter and receive 2 FREE books http://amzn.to/2shQ9Ym

PREVIEW 15 BRIDES OF THE WILD WEST

A 15 book box set with one brand new book, read on for a preview.

Jonny Peterson let out a long breath. He had finally arrived in Lincoln, and it felt like a blessing. An image of blood filled his mind, but he pushed it away with a shake of his head. The journey had been hair-raising, to say the least. When you had to run from home, the last thing you needed was to end up in the middle of a stagecoach robbery. There again, he guessed that was the last thing anyone needed!

Jonny picked up his suitcase, trying not to look at the bullet-ridden body of the man who had been in the carriage with him. Two cowboys loaded the body of Mr. Cormack onto a cart and covered it with a blanket. In Jonny's mind, they seemed too comfortable with the process. Maybe this town was rougher than he thought? It didn't matter, he would only stay as long as needed. Pulling his eyes away he thanked the Lord that it was not him and hurried out of the station.

A blast of wind hit him, he shuddered. It was colder than he had expected even for the time of year. Jonny shrugged against the wind and turned up his collar. walking away he ignored the growl from his stomach. It may want food, but Jonny had nothing on him, only a few coins in the money bag at his waist… it wasn't enough, he couldn't stop to look for food.

He needed to find the man he was seeking as soon as he could. That thought took away the hunger. It looked like he had been given an opportunity, it was one he would be sure not to miss. After what he had heard in the carriage, it seemed as if fate or the Lord had smiled on Jonny and he was determined to make the most of the situation. A wry smile crossed his lips the misfortune of his traveling companion could turn out most fortunate for him.

Picking up his pace he asked for directions and found the pastor's house on the same grounds as the church. It looked a little forlorn, standing at the edge of the cemetery. For a moment, he stood and stared, for the boneyard was densely populated with several white crosses. Too many of them looked new. Jonny tried not to look at them as he hurried on towards the house. A tall, thin man with jet-black hair cut short and real neat came loping out of the house. Almost skipping down the steps and making his way toward the church. Jonny quickened his pace.

"Pastor Philson?"

The man stopped and turned, giving him that pleasant look Jonny saw on many clergymen when they were meeting strangers.

"Yes? How many I help you?"

"I believe you're expecting me." Jonny mentally crossed his fingers. "I'm Jonny Cormack."

Pastor Philson's expression turned to one of recognition, his eyes widening.

"Mr. Cormack, of course, now please call me Phil or Pastor." He shook Jonny's hand firmly. "Glad you could get here."

"I nearly didn't. There was an attempted robbery on the way."

"I'm so sorry. Did you say attempted?"

"The driver and guard managed to get us away." Jonny's stomach twisted. "But not before my companion was killed."

Pastor Philson looked sympathetic and made the sign of the cross.

"It's such a shame. There is so much greed in the world that sometimes I despair."

Jonny silently agreed. His not so lucky companion had been full of greed and disdain for his fellow humans, especially women. Jonny hoped he wouldn't come across the same way.

Pastor Philson ushered him back towards his house.

"Would you like to come in? You look like you're ready to sit down."

"Please."

Jonny went gladly. He was ready to sit down and eat a meal; he hadn't eaten in three days and hadn't slept properly in four. Both of those were in the cards for him, depending on when he got finished with the pastor. The man had promised to help out, so Jonny was going to make sure that things were going to go smoothly.

Apparently, there was a lot of money in being a marriage agent. Jonny hoped it would be quick money. Right now he just needed to make sure things were going to go to plan and that he wouldn't get stuck in a situation he couldn't get out of. If his past caught up with him, he would need to run and fast. A little quick money would go a long way to help with that.

The two men entered the house, which was of simple tastes with a fire still going in the grate. Pastor Philson poured a drink, nearly filling the tumbler to the brim. Jonny raised his eyebrows and regarded this with amusement.

"I thought clergymen weren't allowed to drink."

"Technically, pastors are allowed." Philson grinned. "Besides, I don't drink. But it doesn't mean you can't. You look like you need it."

He handed the glass to Jonny, who took the drink gratefully. The whiskey burned its way down his throat, but that didn't stop him from downing it in one go. Wheezing as it melted his insides, Jonny settled back against the cushions. Suddenly he felt exhausted.

Philson sat on the other couch.

"So, when are the girls arriving?"

For a moment Jonny wondered what he was talking about. Then he remembered. The girls. The ten girls from an orphanage in Atlanta who were looking for love and new lives. His job, or more precisely it had been Jonny Cormack's job. For a moment he felt his stomach turn, but he had to put that behind him. What were the odds that two men who looked similar, had the same first name and could end up sat next to each other? When Cormack died, it seemed like fate and Jonny was more than happy to accept the job of marrying the ten women, with the help from Philson. Together they were to find each girl a husband and marry them as soon as possible. Then he would be paid for the marriage and Jonny could be on his way with cash to spare.

A hand went to his head, and he rubbed his brow. He needed as much money as he could make before he disappeared... and he needed it quickly.

"In three days." Jonny hoped his information was correct. He then remembered the letters and looked embarrassed. "Listen, I've been thinking. Some of the things I wrote regarding them may not have been appropriate. I want to apologize for that and ask for your help."

Philson smiled and shrugged.

"There's no need to apologize if you are truly sorry. However, it happens all the time. Men are desperate for wives and women are in short supply around these parts. Agents like you see a money-making scheme and you bring the girls here to be married off and pocket the fee. I don't like it, but it's not my place to judge." Philson chuckled and raised an eyebrow. "You're the first person who's apologized for it."

Jonny winced. He had no idea that marriage agents were this cruel. Only he wasn't a cruel man. Desperate maybe but not cruel and he wanted to make sure people knew that. Pastor Philson was the best person to start with on that score.

"Well, I know I said something about letting them fend for themselves once they get here. That was harsh." He shifted uncomfortably. "I shouldn't be leaving them to the wolves.

After all, they're meant to come here for a better life, not one that is worse, so I want to see that they are looked after."

"Did you hit your head on the way over here, Mr. Cormack? Because your approach right now is completely different to what you wrote to me before."

Jonny felt heat hit his cheeks and winced at the name Cormack. He must remember it was his name now if he wanted to pull this off. Cormack was dead, and he had left an opportunity for Jonny to earn some running money, only he didn't want to go into things too much. The more he talked about this, the more likely it was he would make a mistake. A smile crossed his face, if he had acted like this Jonny Cormack when his ma and sister were around, they would've paddled his butt, even though he was a grown man. To them that didn't matter as long as you were respectful of others.

Swiftly, he changed the subject.

"I know it's short notice but would you be able to help fix them up with accommodation? It's the least I can do. I haven't been able to do that myself yet as I don't know the area." He decided not to mention that he couldn't afford it.

"Of course not. My housekeeper's sister owns a boarding house. They'll have plenty of room." Philson tilted his head to one side. "Would you like the girls to have employment as well? Just in case they don't get married quickly."

"If that's possible. It will give them time to find the right man." Why had he just said that? The quicker they were married, the better.

Jonny hoped this wouldn't become a long-term investment. If he was lucky, he could get them all married off within a month, if not a couple of weeks. Then he could take what he was owed and leave. He couldn't afford to stay still for very long.

Philson was giving him a funny look.

"Are you sure you're the same Jonny Cormack who wrote letters to me about help getting the girls husbands and gleaning as much money as you can off them? I didn't like that man."

Jonny realized he had to be careful he didn't give himself away. The pastor came across as a nice, genial man who didn't suffer fools gladly.

"I'm the same man. Just had a change of heart." He swallowed and hoped he wouldn't get caught out. "Bereavement does that to you."

"I'm sorry." Philson's expression softened. "Who did you lose?"

"My brother." That was close enough, but Jonny wasn't going to go into it. "Will you help me, Pastor?"

"Of course." Nate stood and held out a hand. "Give me the names and everything you have on them. I'll see what I can do."

"That's all I could ask for."

Jonny fished out the documents from the satchel he carried and handed them over. The pastor disappeared into a room, Jonny guessed it was his study, and closed the door. Taking his glass, Jonny went over to the table where the whiskey was sitting and poured himself another drink. Then he looked to the skies.

"Jonny Cormack, you were one complete beast," he muttered under his breath. "Maybe these girls are lucky you're dead."

Find out if the ladies are better off in **15 Brides of the Wild West – A Brides Cowboys and Babies Box Set** now on SALE for a limited time at $0.99 or FREE ok Kindle Unlimited. Includes a brand new never before published romance.

MORE BOOKS BY INDIANA WAKE

To receive two free Mail Order Bride Romance join Fair Havens Books exclusive newsletter. http://eepurl.com/bHou5D

All Books are FREE on Kindle Unlimited

Newest Books

15 Brides of the Wild West – A Brides Cowboys and Babies Box Set

Trinity's Loss

Hearts Head West

No Going Back

A Baby to Heal his Heart

For the Love of the Baby

A Father's Blessing

A Surprise Proposal

Mail Order Brides Out of Time

Blackmailed by the Rancher

For Love or Duty

The Baby and the Beast.

Saving the Twins

A Dream Come True

Box Sets

15 Brides of the Wild West – includes never before published book.

36 cowboys and Brides Mega Box Set with 5 never before published books.

22 Book Mega Box Set – 22 Brides Ride West for Love

22 Book Mega Box Set – 22 Frontier Brides – Love & Hope Ride West http://amzn.to/1Xf8xNR

16 Book Boxed Set Love & Hearts http://bit.ly/1kXbkw4

10 Frontier Brides and Babies 10 Book Mega Box Set

10 Book Box Set 10 Healing Hearts

7 Brides for 7 lonely Cowboys box set http://amzn.to/1SXaQVG

An English Rose in Texas 5 Book Set 2 books never before published http://amzn.to/1Tl64iH

The Mail Order Bride and the Marriage Agent Series:

The Mail Order Bride and the Stolen Baby

Secret's Lies and a New Family

The Right Choice

The Mail Order Bride and the Hunted Man

His Golden Angel

Mistaken Trust

Love at Eighty Yards

The Narrow Escape

2 Book Set – A Celebration of life & No Sympathy

Based on a True Story

2 Book Special Into the Unknown& Call of the Hunter

Novel Length books

Christmas Hope & Redemption

Strength from Within – Anabella

The Wrong Proposal – Evelyn

A Leaf on the Breeze - Amelia

Nancy and Claudine Love Will Find You

Indiana Wake was born in Denver Colorado where she learned to love the outdoors and horses. At the age of eleven, her parents moved to the United Kingdom to follow her father's career.

It was a strange and foreign new world and it took a while for her to settle down. Her mom raised horses and Indiana soon learned to ride. She would often escape on horseback imagining she was back in the Wild West. As well as horses, Indiana escaped into fiction and dreamed of all the friends she had left behind.

From an early age, she loved stories. They were always sweet and clean and more often than not, included horses, cowboys and most importantly of all a happy ever after. As she got older, she would often be found making up her own stories and would tell them to anyone who would listen.

As she grew up, she continued to write but marriage and a job stole some of her dreams. Then one day she was discussing with a friend at church, how hard it was to get sweet and clean fiction. Though very shy about her writing Indiana agreed to share one of her stories. That friend loved the story and suggested she publish it on kindle. Together they worked really hard and the rest, as they say, is history.

Indiana has had multiple number one bestsellers and now

makes her living from her writing. She believes she was truly blessed to be given this opportunity and thanks each and every one of her readers for making her dream come true.

Belle Fiffer is not your ordinary girl. She grew up in the west where she loved to ride horses and walk in the wilds. At fifteen, she moved to England when her father's job took him across the pond. Leaving behind all her friends she lost herself in books and if she is honest she fell in love with food. She is not ashamed of her curves and loves stories about good, honest men that love their women on the large side.

As a committed Christian, her books are clean, sweet and inspirational. Belle hopes you enjoy the books.

Made in United States
Troutdale, OR
06/11/2024

20475464R00072